Storytime Stretchers

Tongue Twisters, Choruses, Games, and Charades

Naomi Baltuck

August House Publishers, Inc.
ATLANTA

Published 2007 by August House Publishers, Inc.,
3500 Piedmont Road NE, Suite 310, Atlanta, GA 30305
404–442–4420
http://www.augusthouse.com

Book design by Liz Lester

Manufactured in the United States
10 9 8 7 6 5 4 3 2 1 HC
10 9 8 7 6 5 4 3 2 1 PB

LIBRARY OF CONGRESS CATALOGING-IN-PUBLICATION DATA

Baltuck, Naomi, 1956–
    Storytime stretchers : tongue twisters, choruses, games, and
charades / Naomi Baltuck.
        p.   cm.
    Includes bibliographical references and index.
    ISBN-13: 978–0-87483–804–6 (hardcover : alk. paper)
    ISBN-10: 0–87483–804–5 (hardcover : alk. paper)
    ISBN-13: 978–0-87483–805–3 (pbk. : alk. paper)
    ISBN-10: 0–87483–805–3 (pbk. : alk. paper)
  1. Storytelling. 2. Activity programs in education.
  3. Games with music. 4. Singing games. 5. Tongue twisters.
  6. Riddles. 7. Jokes. I. Title. II. Title: Story time strechers.
    LB1042.B346 2007
    372.67'7—dc22   2006030720

The paper used in this publication meets the minimum
requirements of the American National Standards for
Information Sciences—Permanence of Paper for Printed
Library Materials, ANSI.48–1984.

CONTENTS

Knee Slappers, Rib Ticklers, and Tongue Twisters

INTRODUCTION

"I love a riddle, I love a rhyme, I love a singsong any old time."
—Traditional folksong

This book is for storytellers, educators, librarians, camp counselors, parents, and the children whose lives they touch. Their enthusiastic response to my previous collection, *Crazy Gibberish and Other Story Hour Stretches*, demonstrates the continuing need for those songs, stories, and games that encourage playful and thoughtful interaction between people.

These activities transform programs into play parties, listeners into participants, a moment of time into a timeless moment. Best of all, whether you are working with preschoolers or high schoolers, a story stretcher is a great way to create immediate rapport with your audience and within your group.

Music is included for many of the stretchers, but you don't need musical talent—just enthusiasm—to lead any size group through the hand and foot motions, call and response, echo songs, and snappy choruses. I have also included practical tips on body movement, audience management, and how to introduce the stretchers to your group.

Teachers can use them to raise or lower the level of energy in the classroom, to complement a unit of study, or simply to inject spontaneous fun into the day. Camp counselors and Scout leaders can use them to create joyful noise and a feeling of community within their groups. Parents can present them as "love gifts" to their children. Storytellers can dole them out like "storytelling candy," delicious fun in one quick bite. These sweet treats will engage even the toughest audience while adding spice, variety, and balance to a program.

I have included stretchers from my childhood, material from my teaching and camp counseling days, as well as a few learned from other storytellers. Lately, though, my favorite story stretchers are those brought home from school or Girl Scout camp by my own children. Some of these gems I have never seen in print, nor can I find a written source for them, but they are all tried and true.

I hope that this book will recall the days when you skipped rope on the playground chanting, "Cinderella, dressed in yella . . . ," or crowded into a tent in the backyard to tell scary stories with your friends, or giggled with delight while trying to master tongue twisters too colorful to print.

The words and the music might evolve as they are passed from one generation to the next, but kids are still the same. They are movers and shakers, and will always be ready at a moment's notice to rise up singing. If you work or play with children, you can be ready for that moment. Simply use one of these "two-minute miracles" to reach out and welcome them into your singsong circle.

If You Can't Carry a Tune In a Bucket

Chants, Poems, and Other Nonmusical Fun

Let Me See Your Frankenstein

AUDIENCE:
Kindergarten through middle school

TIME:
2 to 3 minutes, depending on the number of verses you use

Leader:	Let me see your Frankenstein!
Group:	What's that you say?
Leader:	I said, "Let me see your Frankenstein!"
Group:	What's that you say?
All:	I said, "Ooh, ah-ah-ah.
	"Ooh, ah-ah-ah.
	"Ooh, ah-ah-ah, ooh!"
Leader:	One more time now!
All:	"Ooh, ah-ah-ah.
	"Ooh, ah-ah-ah.
	"Ooh, ah-ah-ah, ooh!"
Leader:	Let me see your Tarzan!
Group:	What's that you say?
Leader:	I said, "Let me see your Tarzan!"
Group:	What's that you say? (*etc.*)

This call and response stretcher is popular with all ages; younger children love the action, while the friendly satire is especially appreciated by the upper grades. Your audiences will anticipate with delight each new verse. Some of the verses will date this stretcher, but it continues to adapt to current popular culture. I changed the Farrah Fawcett verse to Britney Spears, as today's youngsters have probably never heard of Farrah Fawcett. Britney is now ancient history, so my daughter suggested that we use Lindsay Lohan.

Almost any action associated with a particular character, which you can do first on one side, then the other, will fit into the format of this stretcher. Remember to use your voice. Make your Frankenstein's "oohs and ahs" deep and gruff; make your Lindsay Lohan's ultra-feminine.

I invented the Mr. Spock and the Girl Scout verses to use with my troop. When I was a summer camp director, back in the '80s, we broke with the right-left format to invent a Zorro verse. With an invisible sword, we lunged straight forward on "ooh," and on the "ah-ah-ah," we drew three lines to form a "Z." Have fun making up your own verses.

ACTIONS

Frankenstein! *(Extend both arms in front, like Frankenstein's monster.)*

Ooh *(With elbow locked and arm extended, give right arm a little shake.)*

Ah-ah-ah *(Move left arm three times, once on each "ah.")*

Ooh *(Shake stiff right arm once.)*

Ah-ah-ah *(Move left arm three times, once on each "ah.")*

Ooh *(Shake right arm once.)*

Ah-ah-ah *(Shake left arm three times, once on each "ah.")*

Ooh! *(Give extended right arm one shake.)*

Tarzan *(Beat chest with fists, right, left-left-left.)*

King Tut *(Turn sideways and make like an Egyptian, right, left-left-left.)*

Richard Nixon *(Make the V for victory sign, right, left-left-left.)*

Lindsay Lohan *(Pat hair, right, left-left-left.)*

Rocky Balboa *(Boxing, punch right-left-left-left.)*

Girl Scout *(Make the three-fingered Girl Scout hand sign, right, left-left-left.)*

John Travolta *(Saturday Night Fever disco pose, facing right, left-left-left.)*

Mr. Spock *("Live long and prosper" hand greeting. If you're really talented, you can raise your right and left eyebrows in sync, too!)*

STORYTELLER'S TIP:

Storyteller Katie Knutson told me that she learned this stretcher as a march. The verses in her version have an identical rhythm to my version, but the leader precedes each verse with, "And . . . we're . . . MARCHING!" After each verse, the leader calls, "Back in line now!" What a terrific way to keep a group of kids on a field trip entertained on the way to the bus stop!

The Rabbits Are Eating the Tomatoes!

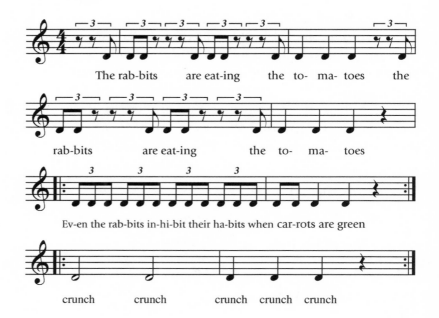

The rabbits are eating the tomatoes.

The rabbits are eating the tomatoes.

Even the rabbits inhibit their habits when carrots are green.

Even the rabbits inhibit their habits when carrots are green.

Crunch, crunch, crunch, crunch, crunch.

Crunch, crunch, crunch, crunch, crunch!

STORYTELLER'S TIP:

This is a great story stretcher to accompany a Br'er Rabbit story.

This stretcher is lively and humorous, with a compelling rhythm. It is a lovely way to introduce a group to the round. The words are simple, and there is no complicated melody to learn. Even kindergartners can enjoy this piece as part of a mixed audience, with older children to help keep the younger ones on track.

Run through all three parts with the audience; twice is usually all it takes. When you feel the group is ready, try it once all together, then divide the audience into groups of three, and do it as a round. When the first group finishes the first two-line verse, the next group begins, and at the end of the next two lines, the third group jumps in. It makes for a very joyful noise, and your audience will feel so accomplished!

One Hen, Two Ducks

Leader: One hen.

Group: One hen.

Leader: One hen, two ducks.

Group: One hen, two ducks.

Leader: One hen, two ducks, three squawking geese.

Group: One hen, two ducks, three squawking geese.

. . . four Limerick oysters.

. . . five corpulent porpoises.

. . . six pairs of Don Alverso's tweezers.

. . . seven thousand screaming Macedonians in full battle array.

. . . eight brass monkeys from the ancient sacred crypts of Egypt.

. . . nine sympathetic, apathetic, diabetic old men on roller skates.

. . . ten iridescent, effervescent, adolescent wombats from the local chapter of the Daughters of the British Empire.

STORYTELLER'S TIP:

This is one you want to be well versed in before you introduce it to an audience, so practice at home first.

This stretcher is truly a stretcher, but never be afraid to challenge your audience. Your listeners will rise to the occasion or go down laughing. Give no warning of the increasing difficulty of this cumulative story stretcher. Simply begin, "Repeat after me . . ."

If you are working with a school or camp group over a period of time, you can let the kids invent verses of their own. My friend Carol Ranck learned this stretcher from her band teacher over thirty years ago, but she couldn't remember the tenth string of nonsense, or whether there even was one. My daughters and I felt that there should be one more, just to round it off. We had fun coming up with a grand finale, which we now use to conclude the stretcher. Inventing their own versions of this stretcher can be especially fun for kids with whom you work regularly.

Zelda's Hammer

AUDIENCE:
Preschool
through
third grade

TIME:
2 minutes

Zelda pounds with one hammer, *(Pantomime hammering with one hand.)*

one hammer, one hammer.

Zelda pounds with one hammer,

then she pounds with two. *(Hold up two fingers.)*

Zelda pounds with two hammers, *(Pantomime hammering with two hands.)*

two hammers, two hammers.

Zelda pounds with two hammers,

then she pounds with three. *(Hold up three fingers.)*

Zelda pounds with three hammers, *(Pantomime hammering with two hands and one foot.)*

three hammers, three hammers.

Zelda pounds with three hammers,

then she pounds with four. *(Hold up four fingers.)*

Zelda pounds with four hammers, *(Pantomime hammering with two hands and two feet.)*

four hammers, four hammers.

Zelda pounds with four hammers,

then she pounds with five. *(Hold up five fingers.)*

STORYTELLER'S TIP:

If you enjoy using music, these words can be sung to the tune of "Did You Ever See a Lassie?"

Zelda pounds with five hammers, *(Pantomime hammering with all four limbs and moving head up and down.)*

five hammers, five hammers.

Zelda pounds with five hammers,

then she takes a break! *(Gently slide to floor, rest head on hands, and pretend to sleep.)*

This cumulative action play is great fun. It won't take long for the children to catch on and chime in. Once you start each motion, continue doing it throughout the stretcher, except for the one line at the end of each verse, where you hold up a finger for each hammer. You can really ham it up, using facial expressions to build the moment as you get busier and busier. You can do this stretcher sitting or standing. If you sit in a chair and move all four limbs up and down at once, the effect is quite comical. If the children are sitting on the floor, make sure before you begin that they have enough room to sit with both hands and feet in front of them, so that no fingers are accidentally stepped on.

Does Anyone Know?

Where can you buy a cap for your _____ ?(*knee*)

Or a key for a lock of your _____? (*hair*)

Can you call your eyes an academy
because there are _____ (*pupils*) there?

What jewels can be found
on the crown of your _____? (*head*)

What crosses the bridge of your ___? (*nose*)

If you wanted to shingle the roof of your _____ (*mouth*)
could you use the nails of your _____? (*toes*)

Can you sit in the shade
of the palm of your _____ (*hand*)
or beat on the drum of your _____? (*ear*)

Can you eat the corn that grows on your _____? (*toe*)

Well, why not grow corn in your _____? (*ear*)

Can the crook in your elbow
be locked up in _____? (*jail*)

If so, just what did it do?

Where can I sharpen my shoulder ___? (*blades*)

I'll be darned if I know. Do YOU?

Reciting this poem is a fun game that also demonstrates the complexity of the English language. As you recite this poem, pause before each missing word, and the kids will chime in the answer. For each of the blanks, you can give the kids a hefty clue by pointing to the corresponding body part.

Uncle Joshua

"Uncle Joshua died last night."

"That's too bad! How did he die?"

"With one eye shut and his mouth awry,

one foot held high and waving goodbye!"

AUDIENCE:
Third through
sixth grades

TIME:
5 to 7 minutes,
depending on
the number of
participants

This cumulative stretcher is doled out by the group leader one action at a time. The play travels around a circle, with everybody either sitting or standing.

To begin, tell the group, "I have unfortunate news to share." Turn to your right-hand neighbor and say, "Uncle Joshua died last night." Then tell him, "Now you say, 'That's too bad! How did he die?'" Wait for your neighbor to repeat the phrase, then tell the group, "I will not only tell him; I'll SHOW him." You respond, "With one eye shut." Have your neighbor pass on the sad news to his neighbor, who will pass the news on to her neighbor and so on.

Leader: "Uncle Joshua died last night."

Neighbor: "That's too bad! How did he die?"

Leader: "With one eye shut . . ." (*Leader shuts one eye and keeps it shut.*)

First neighbor: "Uncle Joshua died last night."

Second neighbor: "That's too bad! How did he die?"

First neighbor: "With one eye shut . . ." (*First neighbor shuts one eye and keeps it shut.*)

STORYTELLER'S TIP:

This is great for
Halloween. In fact, some
versions begin, "The Old
Witch is dead . . ." This
stretcher can also be used
as an icebreaker: by the
last round, everyone is
reduced to giggles. Each
time the play comes back
to the leader, she can pick
up the pace by talking
faster and responding
more quickly in her
exchange with her
neighbor. When the
final round comes back
to the leader, she can
conclude the game with
an emphatic, "May he
rest in peace!"

Around the circle it goes, until everybody has one eye shut. The leader then repeats the rhyme from the beginning, adding the next phrase, "and his mouth awry." Again it travels around the circle until everyone has an eye shut and a twisted mouth, and so on, until everyone has one eye shut, mouth awry, one foot held high, and is waving goodbye.

Tell It With Me

Audience
Participation
Stories

Montana Tex

AUDIENCE:
Kindergarten through sixth grade

TIME:
10 minutes

Back in the days when horses raced like the wind, when sunsets were for riding into, and only the good guys got to wear white hats, there lived a cowboy named **Montana Tex**. He was, of course, a good guy, because he wore a white hat. **Montana Tex** never went anywhere without his pearl-handled six-shooter, **Montana Six**. But his most faithful companion and best friend was his trusty horse, **Giddyup**.

They were very happy riding the range together. In fact, the two of them would probably have lived happily ever after, if not for that nefarious banker **Seymour Cash**. He held the mortgage on **Giddyup**.

One fateful day, that dastardly white-collar criminal **Seymour Cash**, said, "I'm calling in your loan, cowboy. If you don't make your horse payment by noon tomorrow, I will repossess your horse."

Montana Tex didn't know what to do. He was dead broke, without a red cent to his name, because he had just sent his entire life savings back east to pay for an operation for his **mother**. He was standing in the local saloon drinking a glass of warm milk when in came the local mountain woman, **Trapper Sue**. She said, "Why so morose, **Montana Tex**?"

"Because," he replied, "**Seymour Cash** is going to repossess my horse if I can't come up with two hundred dollars by noon tomorrow."

"Two hundred dollars!" exclaimed **Trapper Sue**. "Why, that is the exact amount of the reward offered for **Big Bogue Bill**!"

"**Big Bogue Bill**?"

"Yes, **Big Bogue Bill**! He's wanted dead or alive. He robs the stagecoach every day at about this time. If you left now, you'd have just time enough to catch him!"

"That's a swell idea, **Trapper Sue**!"

He ran out of the saloon and whistled for his horse (who always came when he was called). He leapt into the saddle in a single bound and went galloping off on **Giddyup**. Sure enough, just outside of town, holding up the stagecoach, was **Big Bogue Bill**.

Montana Tex said, "**Big Bogue Bill**, I'm taking you in. Now reach for the sky." And he whipped out **Montana Six**.

"Well," said **Big Bogue Bill**, "it looks like you got the drop on me, **Montana Tex**. Say, that's a good-looking horse ya got there. What's his name?"

Montana Tex told him. His horse, thinking he meant "**giddyup**," took off racing like the wind. **Montana Tex** was left sitting in the dust, staring up into the barrel of a gun held by **Big Bogue Bill**.

"Haw! Now it looks like I got the drop on you!" said **Big Bogue Bill**.

"Well, shoot!" said **Montana Tex**.

"If you insist," said **Big Bogue Bill**.

"Hold it right there!" said **Trapper Sue**. She stepped out from behind a rock and said, "It kinda looks like *I* got the drop on *you*, **Big Bogue Bill**!"

"Well, shoot!" said **Big Bogue Bill**.

"Don't tempt me," said **Trapper Sue**.

They took **Big Bogue Bill** directly to the sheriff's office. They did not pass 'Go,' but they did collect two hundred dollars in reward money. They took it to the bank, and used it to make the final horse payment to that scoundrel **Seymour Cash**.

As they left the bank, **Trapper Sue** said, "I got just one question for you, **Montana Tex**. All the posters said 'Dead or alive.' Why didn't you just plug that lowdown sneakin,' thievin,' cussin,' cattle-rustlin' dirty dog when you had the chance?"

"Well, **Trapper Sue**, seein' as how you just saved my skin, I guess you got a right to know. **Montana Six** isn't really a six-shooter. It's a custom-made pearl-handled six-squirter."

"A squirt gun? **Montana Six** is a squirt gun? But why?"

"Because, my **mother** always told me it wasn't nice to shoot people, and I always listen to my **mother**. Thanks again for helpin' me out. Shucks, **Trapper Sue**, you're a pretty good guy, for a girl!"

Trapper Sue said, "**Montana Tex**, you're a pretty good guy yourself. Now, let's go find your horse."

So **Montana Tex** and **Trapper Sue** walked off into the sunset. They found **Giddyup,** and the three of them lived happily ever after, of course!

Approach this audience participation story with a sense of humor. Be melodramatic in your delivery. Begin by introducing the characters one by one, explaining that everyone in your audience will get to play each part. All they have to do is perform the following actions and make the proper sound each time that particular character is mentioned.

Montana Tex: *Grin and wave to the audience, and say, "Aw, shucks!"*

Giddyup: *Make a galloping noise by slapping your hands on your thighs.*

Seymour Cash: *Rub fingers together greedily, while laughing snidely, "Heh-heh-heh!"*

Trapper Sue: *Throw right fist up into the air and holler with enthusiasm, "Yahoo!"*

Big Bogue Bill: *Make the sound of clearing your throat and pretend to spit out of the side of your mouth.*

Montana Six: *Make a popping sound with finger in cheek.*

Mother: *Clasp hands over heart and lovingly sigh, "Ahhh!"*

In a Dark, Dark Wood

It was a dark dark night, there was a dark dark wood

Ooo- ooo- ooo— And in that dark dark wood there was a

dark dark house Ooo- ooo- ooo—

Ooo— ooo— ooo— ooo— ooo— — —

AUDIENCE:
Kindergarten through sixth grade

TIME:
3 minutes

Leader: It was a dark, dark night.
There was a dark, dark wood.

Group: Ooooooooo . . .

Leader: And in that dark, dark wood there was a dark, dark house.

Group: Oooooooo.
OOOOOOooooooOOOOOooooo . . .

Leader: And in that dark, dark house there was a dark, dark hall.

Group: Ooooooooo . . .

Leader: And off that dark, dark hall there was a dark, dark room.

Group: Oooooooo.
OOOOOOooooooOOOOOooooo . . .

Leader: And in that dark, dark room there was a dark, dark closet.

Group: Ooooooooo . . .

STORYTELLER'S TIP:
If you are telling this story to a younger audience, you can downplay the scary ending. But if you are sharing it with a school-age audience, play it up. When you come to the end, lower your voice, leaning into that last line, as though you are about to whisper a juicy secret. Then catch the audience off its guard, shouting the word "GHOST!" while jumping up with a look of shock and terror on your face. Even if they know what to expect, you are sure to make them jump!

Leader: And in that dark, dark closet
was a dark, dark shelf.

Group: Ooooooo.
OOOOOOooooooOOOOOooooooo . . .

Leader: And on that dark, dark shelf
there was a dark, dark box.

Group: Oooooooo . . .

Leader: And in that dark, dark box
there was a **GHOST!**

This is a popular "jump story," but my friend Gene Gousie added original music to encourage audience participation. The audience sings the eerie song of the wind, which helps create a haunting mood. As this story might be familiar to many people, do not introduce it by title, which would immediately bring the end to mind, taking the punch out of the punchline. Begin, "In this story, you play the part of the wind." I sing the part for them and have them repeat it and then sing the second part and have them repeat it. When the melody goes up, sway side to side and upwards. When the music goes down, sway side to side and downwards. The audience will take its cue from your body language.

Skippin' Home From School

CHORUS:

I was skippin' home from school,

skippin' home from school,

skippin' home from school.

There was my mother,

there was my father,

there was my sister,

there was my brother,

and there was Herbie,

the family pet . . .

and he was THIS big.

REFRAIN:

I was skippin' home from school,

skippin' home from school,

skippin' home from school.

There was my mother . . .

there was my father . . .

there was my sister . . .

but where was Brother?

And there was Herbie,

the family pet . . .

and he was THIS big.

AUDIENCE:
Kindergarten
through
middle school

TIME:
3 minutes

REFRAIN

There was my mother . . .
there was my father . . .
but where was Sister?
And there was Herbie,
the family pet . . .
and he was THIS big!

REFRAIN

There was my mother . . .
but where was Father?
And there was Herbie,
the family pet . . .
And he was THIS BIG!

REFRAIN

But where was Mother?
And there was Herbie,
the family pet.
Then Herbie saw me . . .
and he came closer . . .
and even closer . . .
and Herbie BURPED!

And there was Mother,
and there was Father,

and there was Sister,

and there was Brother,

and there was Herbie,

the family pet,

and he was THIS big!

This hilarious story screams for audience participation. It is so easy that you don't even have to teach it. Just begin with, "You can tell this one with me," and nod encouragement when the children chime in. Don't be afraid to ham it up, and remember to build the suspense. Each time you demonstrate to the audience how big Herbie is getting, pause a little longer, make your reaction a little stronger. At the end, when Herbie burps, supply a sound effect, "Brrrrrooooooooopppp!!!" Then pause for dramatic effect, smile in amazement, and begin joyfully, "And there was Mother!"

ACTIONS

I was skippin' home from school (*On "skippin,'" brush right hand over left hand in downward motion. Repeat with each "skippin' home from school."*)

There was my mother (*Begin snapping fingers on "mother," and keep snapping through successive family members.*)

But where was . . . (*Lift up hands, shake head, and shrug in bewilderment.*)

And there was Herbie (*Begin snapping on "Herbie."*)

And he was THIS big (*Stop snapping, show with two fingers that he is about the size of a mouse. Next time, show with two hands that he has grown to the size of a bunny, then a dog. In the last verse, stretch your arms as wide as possible. The very last time, show with your thumb and forefinger that Herbie is once again as small as a mouse.*)

STORYTELLER'S TIP:
Kids love to imagine what kind of creature Herbie is; they picture everything from toothy worms to furry little rodents. If they ask, don't tell. You can always say, "I don't know, but I don't think you're going to find one at PetSmart."

Little Piggy Rap

AUDIENCE:
First grade
through adult

TIME:
4 minutes

Once upon a time there were three little pigs.
They all hung out at their mama's digs.
She cooked, she cleaned, she fed those swine
till she thought she was gonna go out of her mind.
One fine day, she gave 'em the boot.
She sent them out on their own to root.
"Take care of each other, be light on the hoof,
and keep your eyes peeled for the Big Bad Wolf."
        The wolf, the wolf, the Big Bad Wolf!
        Oink. Oink. Oink-oink-oink!

Three little piggies kissed their mama goodbye,
packed up their duds, and left the family sty.
They went wee, wee, wee all down the road,
fixing to rent, buy, or build an abode.
The first little piggy got a loan from his ma,
and built a cute little house all made of straw.
His brother got a deal on a bundle of sticks.
The third little piggy—she invested in bricks.
        In bricks, in bricks, invested in bricks!
        Oink. Oink. Oink-oink-oink!

The pig boys partied in the straw domicile,
cranked up the boom box and went hog wild,
chilled some Dr Pepper, and were popping the cork,
when the Wolf went by and said, "I smell pork."

"Little pigs, little pigs, let me in."

"Not by the hair of our chinny chin chins."

So *not* by the hair of *his* chinny chin chin

he huffed and puffed and blew the house in.

    He blew, he blew, he blew the house in!

    Oink. Oink. Oink-oink-oink!

Two little piggies ran like ham on wheels.

They rang Sis on the cell phone, with the wolf on their heels.

She met 'em at the door with a big high-five,

along came the wolf with his huffy-puffy jive.

"Avon calling!" "Pizza's here!" He used all his tricks.

That hogwash went over like a ton of bricks.

"Little sow, let me in, we'll have some fun."

"In a pig's eye!" she said, and dialed 9-1-1.

    She dialed, she dialed, 9-1-1!

    Oink. Oink. Oink-oink-oink!

Animal Control came and hauled the wolf away.

His new home's in Yellowstone, that's where he'll stay.

So now the wolf is done with all his trouble-makin',

and Mama's happy 'cause her kids are bringing home their bacon.

The moral of this story isn't just for the swine.

It's a pearl of wisdom to always keep in mind.

When the wolf comes knockin,' don't quiver there in fear,

just grab your phone, be quick to squeal, and watch your little rear.

> Your rear, your rear, watch your little rear!
>
> Oink! Oink! Oink-oink-oink!
>
> Yeahhhh!

Kids love an old tale with a new twist, so I wrote this jazzed-up version of a folktale everybody knows. Begin, "Some pigs say 'oink,' some say, 'wee wee wee,' but the pigs in this story say . . ." Demonstrate the nasal grunting sound made by pigs, which is funnier than simply saying "oink." Have the kids practice piggy grunts, then teach them do it in the proper rhythm. Invite them to help you get a beat going, while snapping your fingers to establish a quick, jazzy rhythm.

The Bed Just So

Once there was a tailor who fell asleep over his work every day. He was sleepy all day long . . . because he could not get any sleep at night.

Every night, when he began to fall asleep, someone— or some*thing*—pulled the covers off his bed. And all night long, the tailor thought he heard someone—or some*thing*—grumbling and complaining and stomping around. "This can't go on," the tailor said. And he went to see the Wise Woman.

"I must be witched," he told her.

"No," the Wise Woman said. "If you were witched, your feet would be on backwards, and your hair would be growing upside down. No, your trouble is that a hudgin has come to stay with you."

"A hudgin!" said the tailor. "What should I do?"

"Make a bed for him," the Wise Woman said. "Then he will leave your bed alone."

So the tailor bought a bed for the hudgin. It was a fine high bed made of oak.

"Now," said the tailor, "you have your bed and I have mine. Let's both have a good night's sleep."

But as soon as the tailor began to fall asleep, he heard a voice grumbling and complaining:

> Too high and too hard!
>
> Too high and too hard!

The next night, the tailor made a low bed of fern and feathers.

But as soon as he began to fall asleep, a voice woke him up, grumbling and complaining:

> Too soft and too tickly!
>
> Too soft and too tickly!

AUDIENCE:
Preschool
through
sixth grade

TIME:
4 to 5 minutes

Every day the tailor tried a new bed for the hudgin. Every night the voice woke him up, grumbling and complaining.

When the tailor made a bed in the cupboard, the voice said:

> Too dark and too stuffy!
>
> Too dark and too stuffy!

Then he tried a hammock. But the voice said:

> Too long and too loose!
>
> Too long and too loose!

The tailor built a cradle. The voice complained:

> Too teeter and too totter!
>
> Too teeter and too totter!

The poor tailor could not find a bed to please the hudgin. "I will never get a good night's sleep," thought the tailor. He was very, very tired.

But that night he cracked open a walnut to eat after dinner. He looked at the half walnut shell, and it looked to him like a tiny bed.

"Why not?" the tailor thought. "I have tried everything else."

So he lined the walnut shell with cotton and peach down. He placed a maple leaf atop it for a cover. And he put it on the windowsill.

Soon he heard a happy humming sound. The tailor looked in the shell. There he saw a small dot, no bigger than a mustard seed.

"Ah, that must be the hudgin," said the tailor. He shut his eyes tight to listen. And he heard a contented voice saying:

STORYTELLER'S TIP:
My hudgin's voice is deep and gruff, so that it is even more of a surprise when the hudgin turns out to be so tiny.

34

Just so. Just so.

    I like a bed made just so.

And at last the tailor got a good night's sleep.

    This story is one of those rare gems that appeals to a wide range of ages. Everyone enjoys trying to imagine exactly what a hudgin is. The first time the hudgin speaks, saying, "Too high and too hard!" I ask the audience, "What did it say?" "Too high and too hard!" they answer. The next time the hudgin says, "Too soft and too tickly," I cup one ear with my hand and gesture to the audience, and the members repeat the hudgin's words. After that, your audience will anticipate its part, and be ready to echo the hudgin. At the very end, the pattern changes slightly to come to a very satisfying conclusion.

Leader: Just so.

Group: Just so.

Leader: I like a bed made . . . (*With outstretched hands and an encouraging nod, invite the audience to complete this line.*)

Group: Just so.

The Little Red House

AUDIENCE:
Preschool
through
third grade

TIME:
11 minutes

Once upon a time, there was a little boy. One day he got tired of his toys and his games and his books. He said, "Mom, I don't have anything to do."

"Why don't you go on a treasure hunt?" she suggested.

"What treasure shall I look for?" asked the boy.

"How about a little red house . . . with no door . . . and a STAR inside?"

"That sounds like fun! Where can I find it?" asked the boy.

"Go ask your sister," said his mother.

So the boy went looking for his sister. As he went, he sang himself a song . . .

> Little red house, little red house,
>
> red as a rose, small as a mouse.
>
> It has no door to open wide,
>
> and best of all, there's a star inside!

His big sister was sitting on her bed doing her homework.

Hey, Sis," said the little boy. "Mom told me to ask you, so maybe you know."

"Know what?" asked his sister.

"Where to find a little red house . . . with no doors . . . and a STAR inside."

His sister thought about it. "Well, there IS my old dollhouse in the closet. It's red."

The boy rummaged through her closet and found a button collection, her hoard of leftover candy from Halloween, and a pair of broken roller skates.

"Maybe you'd better let me find it for you," said his sister. While she went to the closet and lifted the dollhouse down from the shelf, she let him eat all her black jellybeans and choose a button to keep.

"Here it is," she told him, setting the dollhouse down on the floor.

"It's little and red," said the boy, "but it has a door." Peering in through the tiny door, he added, "And no star inside, either. Just dolls."

"Go ask Dad," she suggested.

The boy put his new button and the rest of his jellybeans into his pocket, and skipped off to find his father. As he went, he sang his song . . .

> Little red house, little red house,
>
> red as a rose, small as a mouse.
>
> It has no door to open wide,
>
> and best of all, there's a star inside!

The boy found his father in the garage, where he was painting the roof of a little wooden windmill blue. "Dad," said the boy, "I hope you can help me. Mom told me to ask Sis, and Sis told me to ask you."

"What can I do for you, Son?" asked his father.

"Do you know where to find a little red house . . . with no door . . . and a STAR inside?"

"Would a little blue windmill do?" asked his father.

"No, it's got to be a house," said the boy.

"Well," said his father, "the only little house I know is the doghouse."

"No, Dad. The doghouse is green, and it doesn't have a star inside. Just Max."

"Go ask Granddad," suggested his father.

The boy ran next door to his grandparents' house, singing,

> Little red house, little red house,
>
> red as a rose, small as a mouse.
>
> It has no door to open wide,
>
> and best of all, there's a star inside!

The boy's grandfather was sitting on the front porch swing reading the newspaper.

"Granddad," said the boy, "I hope you can help me. Mom told me to ask Sis, Sis told me to ask Dad, and Dad told me to ask you."

"Ask me what?" said Granddad.

"Do you know where I can find a little red house . . . with no doors . . . and a STAR inside?"

"We could build a little house of cards," suggested his grandfather. "I have a deck of cards that is all red on the back, and the house we build won't have a door."

So the boy and his grandfather went inside and found the deck of red playing cards. On the dining room table they built a house of cards three stories high. They were very careful to place the red side of each card facing out. At last they sat back and admired their work. Their house was certainly red, and it was little, and there was no door. But then the boy thought of something.

"Granddad, it has hearts and diamonds, even kings and queens inside, but no star."

"Well, then, how about the birdhouse your dad made me for my birthday? I hung it in the maple tree in the backyard. It's little and red."

"I bet that's it! Thanks, Granddad!" The boy ran out the door and into the backyard. He found the birdhouse hanging from a branch of the tree. The birdhouse was little and red, but there was a tiny round door in the front.

He ran back and told his grandfather, "That's not the one."

"Go ask your grandmother," suggested his grandfather.

So the boy went inside to look for his grandmother. As he went he sang,

> Little red house, little red house,
>
> red as a rose, small as a mouse.
>
> It has no door to open wide,
>
> and best of all, there's a star inside!

He found his grandmother in her studio, painting a picture. "Grandma, I hope YOU can help me find what I'm looking for! Mom told me to ask Sis, Sis told me to ask Dad, Dad told me to ask Granddad, and Granddad told me to ask you. I'm on a treasure hunt. "

"Sounds like you might need a cookie," said his Grandmother, "to keep up your strength."

The little boy definitely agreed. After seven chocolate chip cookies, two glasses of milk, and a little dish of strawberry ice cream, the boy felt strong enough to continue his search.

"Now, what is this treasure you're seeking, dear?" asked his grandmother.

"I'm looking for a little red house . . . with no door . . . and a STAR inside."

His grandmother chuckled. "A little red house with no doors and a star inside? Let me see . . ." She took her picture album out of the cupboard. "Look here, dear. I have a picture of a little red house." She showed him an old photograph. "This was my schoolhouse a long time ago, when I was your age. It was red and little."

"But Grandma, it has a door," said the boy.

His grandmother closed the book and said with a smile, "I think I know the answer you are looking for."

"Tell me, Grandma!"

"I told it to your mother a long time ago, when she was a little girl. I think you should go ask your mother, dear."

The little boy was so excited. He didn't have the answer yet, but now he knew exactly where to find it. He ran home, singing,

> Little red house, little red house,
>
> red as a rose, small as a mouse.
>
> It has no door to open wide,
>
> and best of all, there's a star inside!

The boy ran into his house calling, "Mom! Mom!"

"In the kitchen, dear," called his mother.

STORYTELLER'S TIP:

Have an apple tucked into your purse or pocket. When you get to the end of the story, cut the apple in half crosswise, and show the children the star. The wonder in their eyes is as good as magic, and they will never eat another apple without seeing stars! If you would rather not carry a knife, even a blunt one, pre-cut the apple before you begin your program; a little 7Up or lemon juice will keep an apple from turning brown.

He found her washing apples and handing them to his father, who was peeling them.

The little boy said, "Mom, you told me to ask Sis, Sis told me to ask Dad, Dad told me to ask Granddad, and Granddad told me to ask Grandma. But Grandma said you would know where to find the little red house with no doors and a star inside. Did you know the answer all along?"

His mother smiled and nodded.

"Will you show me?"

She smiled and nodded again. His mother took a shiny red apple and set it on the table in front of the boy.

"Here it is," she said.

"But Mom, that's not a house."

"It could be, if you use your imagination. It's little and it's red, isn't it?"

"Yes," agreed the boy.

"Look here," she said, pointing to the brown stem on top. "It even has a chimney."

"And no door," said the boy. "But what about the star? It should have a star inside."

"Let's take a look inside," said his mother. With a knife she cut the apple in half crosswise. She twisted open the apple and showed him the inside. There was a perfect star formed by the seeds and the core. The boy's eyes opened wide in amazement. There it was! The house was little, it was red, it had no doors, and there was the star!

That was a long time ago. The boy still eats apples. Sometimes he eats them whole and chews around the core. Sometimes he eats his apple in slices. Sometimes he cuts them crosswise and looks at the stars. And when he eats that crisp, sweet apple, you can be sure that he sings himself a little song . . .

> Little red house, little red house,
>
> red as a rose, small as a mouse.
>
> It has no door to open wide,
>
> and best of all, there's a star inside!

I learned this story from Seattle storyteller Sharon Creeden. I added the song, and the cumulative element, to encourage audience participation. I teach the song to the audience the first time the boy sings it in the story. "The little boy began to sing a song. It goes like this." Sing the song and then invite the audience to sing it with you. The next time the little boy is about to sing, ask the audience, "Do you remember how it goes?" and the members will join in. Each time the boy runs to another person for help, he reels off a list of the people he has already approached. As the boy begins, "Mom told me to ask _____," hesitate an instant, and your audience will fill in the blank for you.

The Coffin

AUDIENCE:
*Second grade
through adult*

TIME:
7 minutes

Some people like to be scared. I used to. I used to stay up late and watch scary movies or tell spooky stories with my friends. People get a kick out of that sort of thing—until the day they get a *real* scare. At least, that's what happened to me.

Our house was less than a mile from my middle school. Sometimes I went to the school dances, and then I would walk home with my best friend, Patti Begley. I was glad for her company on those late-night walks home, because in between my school and my house, there was a big graveyard. In broad daylight, I could save ten minutes by cutting across it. But at night, I *always* went around.

The year I was in eighth grade, Halloween fell on a Friday, so the school held a Halloween dance. Patti went as a pirate, and I went as a ghost, in white leotards and a sheet.

After the dance, as Patti and I walked home, we talked about the boys we had danced with and whose costumes we liked best. But the moon was full, there was a chill in the air, and our conversation trailed off. Somebody's dog howled at the moon. Far away, a train whistle shrieked. As we got to the graveyard, we heard the church clock strike eleven.

"Oh, no!" I told Patti. "I'm in trouble! I promised my mom I'd be home by eleven!"

"You could cut across the graveyard," teased Patti. "You're dressed for the part."

"Will you come with me? Please?" I begged.

"Can't," said Patti. "I promised my mom I'd mail a letter on the way to the dance, and it's still here in my purse. If I don't swing by a mailbox, I'm the one who's in trouble."

I looked around, hoping to spot one last trick-ortreater straggling home, maybe even going in my direction. The streets were deserted.

"I'd better just go. If I cut across the graveyard, I can be home in fifteen minutes."

I said goodnight to Patti, and let myself into the graveyard through the tall iron gate.

Huge old oak trees swayed in a chilly wind, their branches forming eerie silhouettes against the streetlights on the far side of the graveyard. Overhead, dead leaves still clinging to the branches rattled against each other. Tree limbs creaked and groaned.

I started walking, listening to the *swish, swish, swish* of dead leaves beneath my feet. I was halfway across the graveyard when . . . *AHHHH!* I nearly fell headlong into a deep hole. I could have broken my neck! My heart was pounding as I caught my breath. I looked closer. It wasn't just a hole . . . it was an open grave, with a pile of fresh dirt heaped beside it, looking like . . . something had just kicked off its covers. It was so deep, I couldn't see to the bottom of it.

"It must be for an early funeral, first thing in the morning," I told myself, but I started walking faster, *swish, swish, swish,* until my feet were really kicking up the dead leaves.

You know how it is when you're taking the garbage out at night or searching for the light switch at the foot of the stairs after you've been sent to the cellar for a can of corn? You get this creepy feeling. It makes the hair on the back of your neck stand on end, and your eyes prickle, and your skin crawl. Well, I got that feeling . . . and walked even faster.

Swish, swish, swish. Swish, swish, swish.

Then, I heard something else. But what was it?

Thump, thump, thump! It was coming from behind me. *Thump, thump, thump!*

I walked as fast as a kid can walk without breaking into a run. At last I got to the far side of the graveyard.

I stepped through the gate, but as I turned to latch it, I couldn't believe my eyes. By the open grave I saw a tall black coffin standing on end. Somehow it had lifted itself out of its grave, and it was coming toward me!

Thump! Thump! Thump!

"The gate will stop the coffin!" I thought as I latched the gate and bolted for home. As I tore down the block, I heard a crash and glanced back in time to see the coffin smash through the fence.

Thump, thump, thump! It hopped awkwardly along the sidewalk after me.

Thump, thump, thump! I raced around the corner onto the next block.

Thump, thump, thump! My house was halfway down the block. If only I could get to my house! As I raced up my front walk, I heard it . . . closer . . . closer.

Thump, thump, thump! I took the porch steps in a single bound. The house was dark inside. Everyone must have gone to bed. Had they left the door unlocked?

Thump, thump, thump! The coffin was at the end of the walk. I tried the door. Yes, it was unlocked! A good thing, too; by the time I slammed the door shut behind me, the coffin was halfway up our front walk. I bolted the door behind me. "The door will stop it!" I thought as I raced up the stairs to the landing.

Thump! CRASH! The front door rattled.

Thump! CRASH! The coffin was throwing itself against the door!

Thump! CRASH! The door was nearly shaken off its hinges!

As I turned and ran, I could hear the door splinter and give way. I ran down the upstairs hall and locked myself in the bathroom.

Thump! Thump! Thump! It was coming up the stairs. The stairs hadn't stopped it!

Thump! Thump! Thump! Down the hall it came.

Thump! Thump! Thump! It stopped outside the bathroom door. I ran to the far end of the bathroom and cowered in the corner.

Thump! CRASH! It was throwing itself against the bathroom door.

Thump! CRASH! Such a flimsy door!

Thump! CRASH! The door broke off its hinges and crashed to the floor. The thing stood in the doorway for an instant, then started toward me.

Thump! Thump! Thump!

I was trapped. Cornered. There was no hope. "MOM!" I screamed.

Then I had an idea. It was my only chance. Frantically I whipped open the medicine cabinet, grabbed a big box of mentholated cough drops, and held them out at arm's length.

Sure enough, *that's* what stopped the coffin!

This story works for a wide age range, and no matter how old or young your audience, there is plenty of room for audience participation. Before you begin, you can invite your audience to help you enhance the telling by providing sound effects. If you wish, you can assign audience members to provide the sound of the wind, the distant whistle of the train, the howling of the dog, the creak of branches overhead. When you get to a place in the telling that requires a sound effect, pause and point to the person who is to provide it. Everyone can mimic the swish of the dead leaves and the thump of the coffin, which I make with the rhythmic stamp of feet.

If people seem hesitant to join in after the first "thump, thump, thump," you can say, "Oh, no, it was much louder than that. Can you help me out?" After they join you in creating a thunderous *"Thump, thump, thump,"* tell them, "Yes! That's just how it was." A stamp and a clap make an effective *"Thump! Crash!"* which your audience can also join in on.

STORYTELLER'S TIP:
Like many camp stories, this one is easily adapted. You can make this story seem more real by telling it as something that actually happened to you. I set it in my middle school years to enhance its appeal to older children. If you are addressing a young audience, you may want to resist the urge to turn this into a "jump story" as you discover the open grave, emphasizing instead the humor and downplaying the scariness. However scary you make it, the silly punch line at the end offers comic relief and dispels tension.

The Dramatic Diagnosis of Doctor Drake

AUDIENCE:
Second
through
six grades

TIME:
7 minutes,
including time
to practice

Once upon a time there was a **duck** *(quack)* who caught a **cold** *(achoo!)*, or what he thought was a **cold** *(achoo!)*. "I must go to a **doctor**," *(clap!)* said the **duck** *(quack!)*. "Which **doctor** *(clap!)* should I see?"

"Try **Doctor Drake**, *(clap! clap!)* advised a friend.

So the **duck** *(quack!)* went to **Doctor Drake** *(clap! clap!)*.

The **doctor** *(clap!)* examined the **duck** *(quack!)*, and looked down his throat. "Just as I suspected! You've got the **epizoodic** *(oh!)*."

"The what?" asked the **duck** *(quack!)*.

"The **epizoodic** *(oh!)*, no more nor less," answered **Doctor Drake** *(clap! clap!)*.

The **duck** *(quack!)* was annoyed. "What a **doctor** *(clap!)*! I'd sooner go to a quack **doctor** *(clap!)*. Even a quack **doctor** *(clap!)* can treat a **duck** *(quack!)* for a common **cold** *(achoo!)*."

"Suit yourself," said **Doctor Drake** *(clap! clap!)*.

So the **duck** *(quack!)* went to see a quack **doctor** *(clap!)*.

"Hmmmm, " said the quack **doctor** *(clap!)*. "Looks like the **epizoodic** *(oh!)*."

"The what?" asked the **duck** *(quack!)*.

"The **epizoodic** *(oh!)*, no more nor less," said the quack **doctor** *(clap!)*.

"Aw, go chase yourself," said the **duck** *(quack!)*. "Don't you think I know a common **cold** *(achoo!)* when I catch one? I'll go to another **doctor** *(clap!)*."

So the **duck** *(quack!)* went to a famous eye, throat, and bill specialist. This **doctor** *(clap!)* made the **duck** *(quack!)* open his mouth and peered into it. "Hmmm!" he said, shaking his head. "It looks like you have the **epizoodic** *(oh!)*."

"The what?" asked the **duck** *(quack!)*.

"The **epizoodic** *(oh!)*, no more nor less," answered the **doctor** *(clap!)*.

"What shall I do?" asked the **duck** *(quack!)*.

"There is only one **doctor** *(clap!)* who can cure the **epizoodic** *(oh!)*," answered the **doctor** *(clap!)*.

"And who is that?" asked the **duck** *(quack!)*.

"**Doctor Drake** *(clap! clap!)*. He is a specialist in the field of the **epizoodic** *(oh!)*. You had better go to **Doctor Drake** *(clap! clap!)*."

So the **duck** *(quack!)* hurried to **Doctor Drake** *(clap! clap!)* as fast as he could waddle. **Doctor Drake** *(clap! clap!)* cured him, of course.

"Thank you, **Doctor Drake**! *(clap! clap!)*" said the duck *(quack!)*. Why, I bet you could even cure the common **cold** *(achoo!)*! How can I ever repay you, **Doctor**? *(clap!)*" asked the **duck** *(quack!)*.

"Don't worry," said **Doctor Drake** *(clap! clap!)*. "I'll send you my bill in the morning."

And that concludes the dramatic diagnosis of **Doctor Drake** *(clap! clap!)*.

Tell your audience, "I need you to clap whenever I say the word 'doctor.' And clap whenever I say the word 'drake.' When I say 'doctor' and 'drake' together, I need you to clap, not once, but twice.

"Whenever I say 'duck,' quack like a duck, like this *(quack!)*. When I say 'cold,' you sneeze *(achoo!)* And when I say 'epizoodic,' you say, 'Oh!' Put this all together, and you have the makings of a riveting DOCudrama, or perhaps it is a DUCKudrama, I'm not sure which."

Doctor: *clap!*

Doctor Drake: *clap! clap!*

Duck: *quack!*

Cold: *achoo!*

Epizoodic: *Oh! (Gasp and clap hands to face in alarm.)*

STORYTELLER'S TIP:

This story is much funnier if you don't say "quack" but actually make a quacking sound, like a duck. Practice with your audience—similar to a quick game of Simon Says, only prompting them with the different word cues— before you begin the actual telling of the story. When your audience gets the hang of it, you can pick up the pace. It is more difficult than it at first appears, but worth the effort, as it sounds quite funny when punctuated with all the quacks.

Night and Day

AUDIENCE:
Preschool
through adult

TIME:
7 to 10 minutes,
depending on
the degree of
participation

A long time ago, when the world was new, and the animals could still talk to each other, there was no difference between night and day. The world was always just the same—dark and gray, dark and gray, dark and gray.

"Croak!" said Frog. "I can't catch a mosquito if I can't see it. We need more light!"

"And I'm always bumping into trees," complained Rabbit.

Buffalo grumbled, "I can't see where to put my feet. I can't tell where the plains end and the mountains begin."

"More light, more light, more light!" they chanted. "More light, more light, more light!"

"WELL, I LIKE IT DARK!" growled Grizzly Bear. "It's just right for taking a good, long nap. And I LIKE a good, long nap!"

"Too much light blinds me," complained Owl.

"And I feel safe in the dark," said Raccoon. "My enemies can't find me."

"More night, more night, more night!" they chanted. "More night, more night, more night!"

The animals argued and argued. Those who wanted more night elected Bear for their leader, because he could talk the loudest. Those who wanted more light chose Frog, because she had bright ideas.

"I know!" said Frog. "Why don't we take turns? First we could have one night, then one day, one night, one day, one night, one day. *Crrrroak!*"

"That's a foolish idea!" said Bear. "I would no sooner be settling in for a good long nap, when the daylight would come and wake me up. I think it should be six months night, one day light. That would be just right."

All the animals began to argue.

"*Crrroak!*" said Frog. "It is clear that there can be no peace on Earth until this matter is decided."

For once, everybody agreed, but how could they decide?

"I know! Why don't we have a contest?" suggested Frog. "The one who can persist in this argument the longest will win."

"I like that idea," said Bear. "With my big voice, I shall surely win. I'LL go first."

Each group gathered round to cheer on its champion. First there were the animals of the night—Raccoon, Owl, Skunk, Bat, Rat, and many more. Then there were the animals who preferred daylight—Eagle, Rabbit, Buffalo, Turtle, Squirrel, and all the others.

The contest began, with the champions of day and night calling out to each other, back and forth, back and forth, back and forth.

Bear thundered: "Six months night, one day light. Six months night, one day light."

Frog answered back: "One night, one day, one night, one day, one night, one day. *Crroak!*"

Hours passed. Bear and Frog were exhausted, but still they argued.

"Six months night, one day light. Six months night, one day light."

"One night, one day, one night, one day, one night, one day. *Crroak!*"

Days passed. Bear's throat was sore from shouting, and even Frog was sounding a little croaky, but still they persisted.

"Six months night, one day light. Six months night, one day light."

"One night, one day, one night, one day, one night, one day. *Crroak!*"

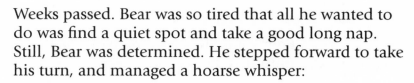

Weeks passed. Bear was so tired that all he wanted to do was find a quiet spot and take a good long nap. Still, Bear was determined. He stepped forward to take his turn, and managed a hoarse whisper:

"Six . . . months . . . night, one . . . day . . . light. Six . . . months . . . night, one . . . day . . . light."

Frog was so tired that even her croaks sounded croakier than usual. But still she persisted.

"One night . . . one day . . . one night . . . one day . . . one night . . . one day . . . *Crroak!*"

Then it was Bear's turn again. He opened his mouth . . . but nothing came out! He had lost his voice. Everyone had to agree that Frog had won the contest.

But Bear was a good loser. He cleared his throat and said, "You won fair and square, Frog. It shall be just as you say: first one night, then one day, one night, then one day. As for me, I am going to find a dark cave somewhere and sleep for as long as I want. Winter is coming, and I'd just as soon sleep right through it. There's only one thing that worries me."

"What's that, Bear?" asked Frog.

"I don't want to oversleep and miss the springtime as well, for I always liked the springtime."

"I know!" said Frog. "You have a good long nap, Bear. Sleep as long as you like. In the springtime, when the flowers are in bloom, my friends and I will wake you."

Bear was delighted with the arrangement. "Thank you, Frog!" Off he went to find a nice dark cave. Frog was as good as her word, and so it is to this day. Grizzly Bear never takes his long winter nap so far from the frog pond that he cannot hear the voices of the frogs calling to wake him in the springtime, when the flowers are bursting into bloom. And even today, the frogs are still talking about the exciting contest between Bear and Frog. If you stand by a frog pond and listen, you can hear the happy chorus of the frogs as they sing out . . .

"One night, one day, one night, one day, one night, one day . . . *Crrroak!*"

This story is one of those rare gems that will work with a very wide age range, from very young children to older children and even adults. You can tell it with as much or as little audience participation as you wish. Since it is very exciting for kids to play an active part in the story, I emphasize and encourage participation, especially with younger audiences.

When Bear speaks in this story, I make him loud and boastful, but in a good-natured way. Frog is quietly confident and determined. When it is time for the champions to compete, I have Bear and Frog pull listeners right into the story. Without skipping a beat, the champions take turns gathering their friends and supporters. In my Bear voice I say, "I need all the creatures of the night to help me win this contest. Who's with me?"

Children in the audience will raise their hands, and I call on them. One might say, "Bat!" "That's right! Bat is with me! Who else?" Someone else might say, "Tiger!" "That's right! Tiger likes the night. Who else?" When every one who wants a turn has been called on, then "Bear" says, "This is our big chance! When it's our turn, here's what we're going to say: 'Six months night, one day light. Six months night, one day light.'" Have them repeat the chant. If the response is weak, just say, "We won't win like that. Let's try it again. Louder!"

Then Frog has her turn to recruit help. "You don't want it to be dark out all the time, do you? Who out there wants more sunshine? Who will help ME out?" The children will raise their hands again, and you can call on them for their answers. "Elephant!" "That's right! Who else likes the daylight?" "Cows!" "Oh, yes, I want the cows on my team, too." When everyone has had a turn, Frog can say, "Now this is what we're going to say . . ." Teach them their refrain: "One night, one day, one night, one day, one night, one day. *Crroak!*"

The contest is lively, and the children will gladly root for both teams, just for the fun of it.

Sing It High, Sing It Low

Action Songs, Musical Games, and Snappy Choruses

Move Over

AUDIENCE:
Kindergarten
through
fifth grade

TIME;
Varies, depending
on the number
of participants

Move over and make room for (child's name) She does-n't take ve-ry much space Since (child's name) is one of our ve-ry best friends we sure-ly can find her a place. Move ov-er, move ov-er, and quick like a rig-gi-ty jig— — — We'll al-ways move ov-er for (child's name), for (child's name) is not ve-ry big. We'll

STORYTELLER'S TIP:

This is a great icebreaker
and a good stretcher to
open a smaller group
session of teaching or
storytelling.

Move over and make room for Elly.

She doesn't take very much space.

Since Elly is one of our very best friends,

we surely can find her a place.

CHORUS

Move over, move over,

and quick like a riggity jig.

We'll always move over for Elly,

for Elly is not very big.

We'll always move over for Elly,

for Elly is not very big.

LAST VERSE

She won't have to stand in the corner.

She won't have to sit on the floor.

We'll always move over for our friends,

and still there'll be room for one more!

This stretcher can be sung, with each child's name inserted in the appropriate places as you go round in a circle: "Move over and make room for _____." It can also be played as a game. The leader can begin by singing a welcome to the first child, and having that child come sit beside her as everyone sings that child's name into the first verse. That child can then choose another child to come and join the circle, with everyone singing a welcome to that child by name. This name game can be played by children who already know each other, or used as a mixer for groups, following brief introductions. When everyone's name has been sung, the leader can conclude by singing the last verse.

Teeter-Totter Woo!

AUDIENCE:
First grade through middle school

TIME:
4 minutes

CHORUS (ALL)

We're singin' in the rain,

just singin' in the rain.

What a glorious feeling, we're . . .

Teeter-totter, teeter-totter, teeter-totter WOO!

Teeter-totter, teeter-totter, teeter-totter WOO!

Teeter-totter, teeter-totter, teeter-totter WOO!

Leader: Uh huh!

Group: Uh huh!

Leader: Oh, yeah!

Group: Oh, yeah!

Leader: Thumbs up!

Group: Thumbs up!

CHORUS (ALL)

We're singin' in the rain,

just singin' in the rain.

What a glorious feeling, we're . . .

Teeter-totter, teeter-totter, teeter-totter WOO!

Teeter-totter, teeter-totter, teeter-totter WOO!

Teeter-totter, teeter-totter, teeter-totter WOO!

Leader: Uh huh!

Group: Uh huh!

Leader: Oh, yeah!

Group:	Oh, yeah!
Leader:	Thumbs up!
Group:	Thumbs up!
Leader:	Elbows back!
Group:	Elbows back!

ADDITIONAL VERSES

Knees together!

Toes together!

Bend down!

Chin up!

Bum out!

Tongue out!

This is one of my favorite story stretchers. Folks think they are going to get a rendition of "Singing in the Rain," but when you launch into your "teeter-totters," with the vaudevillian knee trick, it is a daffy and delightful departure from the expected. Interactive songs help establish a strong connection between a group leader and her audience, and so does throwing off constraints and simply being silly together. By the time you get to the end of this stretcher, believe me, you and your audience will have bonded!

As this is not strictly an echo song, be clear with your instructions. I begin, "You all know the words to 'Singing in the Rain'? We'll sing that together, but only the first couple of lines. But first, try *this.*" Facing the audience, a hand on each knee, and knees bent outward, I move my knees together until they touch, quickly slide my hands to the opposite knees, and bring my knees back out with my arms crossed. I reverse the process, bringing my knees together, switching hands back, and when my knees come away, my arms are uncrossed. You have surely seen this trick in vaudeville comedy acts. Once you get your speed up, it is quite impressive.

STORYTELLER'S TIP:

After singing the last chorus of "Singing in the Rain" (tongue still out), and going through my last series of teeter-totters, I begin the cumulative series of actions one last time and end with, "That's all!"

57

Give audience members only about fifteen seconds to practice the trick; half the fun is bumbling through it together. Tell them that for the next part of the song, you want them to be your echo, and to do what you do. Remember, each time you add another position, hold it throughout the "Singing in the Rain" sequence. When you get to the teeter-totters, do the knee trick, and then start all over again, building up to a greater degree of difficulty and goofiness by adding a new action with each additional verse.

The age recommendations for this dynamic stretcher are general. I would not hesitate to use it with a kindergarten through sixth-grade audience, but for an audience consisting only of kindergartners, I would choose something easier, such as " Zelda's Hammer." I also have had occasion to use this stretcher with adult audiences, with great results.

ACTIONS

Teeter-totter teeter-totter teeter-totter (*With hands on knees, bring knees together, switch hands to opposite knees, and bring out knees with arms crossed. Repeat in time with the music.*)

WOO! (*Straighten up, and throw both hands up, as if surprised.*)

Forty Years on an Iceberg

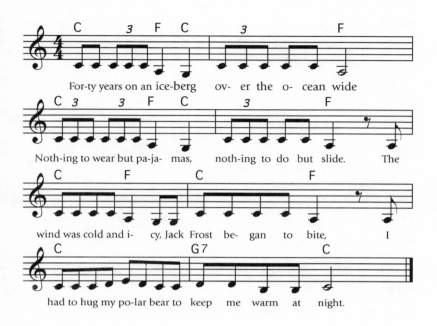

For-ty years on an ice-berg ov- er the o- cean wide

Noth-ing to wear but pa-ja- mas, noth-ing to do but slide. The

wind was cold and i- cy, Jack Frost be- gan to bite, I

had to hug my po-lar bear to keep me warm at night.

Forty years on an iceberg,

over the ocean wide.

Nothing to wear but pajamas,

nothing to do but slide.

The wind was cold and icy.

Jack Frost began to bite.

I had to hug my polar bear

to keep me warm at night.

STORYTELLER'S TIP:
When doing this stretcher
with a group for the first
time, the hug is such a
lovely surprise that you
don't want to give away
the ending. But it does
not hurt to inform your
audience beforehand
that this is a gentle story
stretcher. With a very
young audience, I prefer
to keep it simple, singing
through it once to show
them the hand motions,
and then singing it
through one more
time all together.

In spite of the title, this is a lovely icebreaker with a heart-warming ending. This is so easy to learn that you don't even have to teach it. Just invite your audience to sing along and follow your actions. When you come to the hug at the end of the song, you can hug yourself, or if you are with children you know, and who are comfortable with you, it might feel appropriate to hug your neighbor. Begin by singing the whole song

through. Then sing it through a second time, omitting the first phrase but continuing the actions. The third time through, omit the first and second phrases but continue the actions. By the time you get to the eighth time, you will be doing actions only. Conclude by singing the song aloud one more time, with all the words and all the actions.

ACTIONS

Forty years on an iceberg, *(Hold up ten fingers; open and close four times to indicate forty.)*

over the ocean wide. *(Make waves with hand motion.)*

Nothing to wear but pajamas, *(Slide hands down from head to toes, shaking head sadly.)*

nothing to do but slide. *(Make sliding motion with both hands.)*

The wind was cold and icy. *(Shiver and hug self.)*

Jack Frost began to bite. *(Pluck neighbor's sleeve gently.)*

I had to hug my polar bear to keep me warm at night. *(Hug self or neighbor.)*

Bazooka-zooka Bubble Gum!

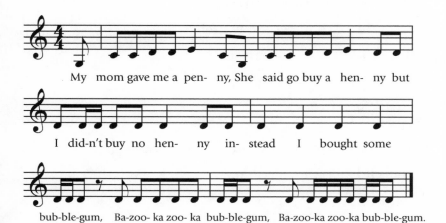

AUDIENCE:
Kindergarten through middle school

TIME:
2 minutes

My mom gave a penny.

She said "Go buy a henny."

But I didn't buy no henny.

CHORUS:

Instead I bought some bubble gum!

Bazooka-zooka bubble gum!

Bazooka-zooka bubble gum!

My mom gave me a nickel.

She said "Go buy a pickle."

But I didn't buy no pickle.

CHORUS

My mom gave me a dime.

She said "Go buy a lime."

But I didn't buy no lime.

CHORUS

My mom gave me quarter.
She said "Go buy some warter."
But I didn't buy no warter.

CHORUS

My mom gave me a dollar.
She said "Go buy a collar."
But I didn't buy no collar.

CHORUS

My mom gave me a Visa.
She said "Go buy a pizza."
But I didn't buy no pizza.

CHORUS

My mom gave me a five.
She said to stay alive.
But I didn't stay alive.

FINAL CHORUS

Instead I choked on bubble gum!
Bazooka-zooka bubble gum!
Bazooka-zooka bubble gum!

STORYTELLER'S TIP:

I often catch the kids' attention by introducing this stretcher with a corny joke, which goes over especially well at a school performance. I ask, "What's the difference between a teacher and a train?" Answer: "A train says, 'Choo-choo' but a teacher says, 'Spit out that gum!'"

This stretcher is popular with kids of all ages. It is peppy and humorous. Older children will especially appreciate the irony of the last verse. The hand motions are easy to follow, and the actions are so easy to catch onto that you don't even have to teach them. Just start singing, and the kids will jump right in.

ACTIONS

My mom gave me (*Point to self.*) . . .

. . . a nickel. (*Hold an imaginary coin.*)

She said "Go buy a pickle." (*Point forefinger in time to music, as if issuing a command.*)

But I . . . (*Point to self.*)

. . . didn't buy no pickle. (*Shake head while indicating "no" by waving finger.*)

Instead I bought some bubble gum! (*Clap as you say "bubble gum!"*)

Bazooka-zooka . . . (*With hands pressed flatly together in front, move them in a circular motion while moving head back and forth.*)

. . . bubble gum! (*Clap again on "bubble gum!"*)

Bazooka-zooka bubble gum! (*Repeat circle hand motion and bobble-head, clapping on "bubble gum!"*)

Road Kill Stew

AUDIENCE:
Second grade
through
middle school

TIME:
4 minutes

Road kill stew, road kill stew,

tastes so good, just like it should.

First you go down to the interstate.

You wait for a critter to meet its fate.

You take it home and you make it great.

Road kill stew, road kill stew.

The gross and goofy humor in this song, set to the tune of "Three Blind Mice," appeals to older kids as well as younger ones. It can be sung in unison by the group or by two or three smaller groups as a round. Before attempting to sing it as a round, sing it through several times. As soon as the first group finishes the line, "Road kill stew, road kill stew," the second group begins, "Road kill stew, road kill stew," and then the third group jumps in.

STORYTELLER'S TIP:

Don't start out too fast, or the group might stumble when it comes to the faster-paced line, "First you go down to the interstate."

The Dickey Bird

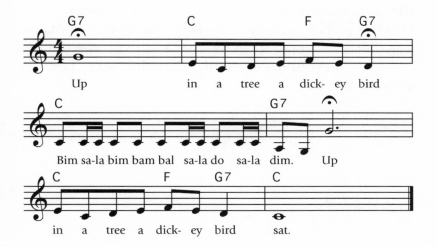

AUDIENCE:
Third through
sixth grades

TIME:
3 minutes

Leader: Up in a tree a dickey bird . . .

Group: Bim sala bim bam bal sala do sala dim.

Leader: Up in a tree a dickey bird *sat.*

Leader: Below him crawled a furry black . . .

Group: Bim sala bim bam bal sala do sala dim.

Leader: Below him crawled a furry black *cat.*

Leader: He said for dinner I shall have . . .

Group: Bim sala bim bam bal sala do sala dim.

Leader: He said for dinner I shall have *you!*

Leader: Then all at once the dickey bird . . .

Group: Bim sala bim bam bal sala do sala dim.

Leader: Then all at once the dickey bird *FLEW!*

STORYTELLER'S TIP:

Don't wait until everyone
has gotten the chorus
down perfectly to try this
song as a group. Children
will pick it up as they go.
Start slowly, and once
they seem to have
grasped it, speed up the
"bim sala bims" while
keeping the same slow,
steady pace for the
verses. The contrast is
comical and will provide
an incentive for the kids
to learn; they will want to
see how fast they can go
before tripping on their
tongues. At the end of
each verse, emphasize
the last word; then pause
for one long second
before launching into the
next verse. The dramatic
effect is worth the wait.

I love this story stretcher for its clever wording, varied pacing, and happy ending. Start out by teaching your audience the challenging chorus, speaking slowly, breaking it down into two parts ("bim sala bim bam" and then "bal sala do sala dim"). Then put them together and try to speed it up. Indicate with your hands exactly when they are to jump in with the chorus.

Sardines!

AUDIENCE:
Second through sixth grades

TIME:
2 minutes

STORYTELLER'S TIP:

Camp counselors and Scout leaders might want to complement this song with a hide-and-seek game called "Sardines." Depending on available space, it can be played indoors or out. The first "sardine" hides, while others cover their eyes and count. After counting to fifty or one hundred, depending on how far the sardine needs to go, it's "Ready or not, here we come!" When someone finds the sardine, she crawls into hiding, too. The trick is to see how many kids can cram into one hiding spot without giggling loud enough to give away their location to the other seekers. The game ends when the last child finds the other sardines. For safety's sake, I always establish a signal to call all the kids out of hiding and report back to me. To serve this purpose, I bring the big yellow plastic bugle I call Old Blew, but a whistle will do the trick.

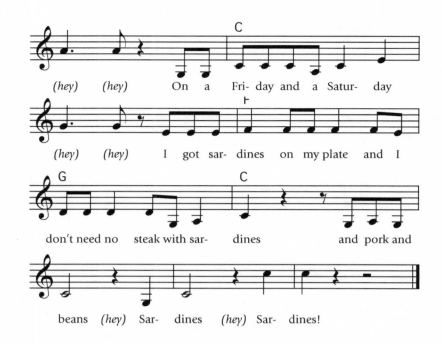

(hey) (hey) On a Fri- day and a Satur- day
(hey) (hey) I got sar- dines on my plate and I
don't need no steak with sar- dines and pork and
beans (hey) Sar- dines (hey) Sar- dines!

Leader:	Sardines!
Group:	Hey!
Leader:	And pork and beans!
Group:	Hey!
All:	Sardines!
Leader:	Every morning by the riverside.
All:	Sardines!
Leader:	See the people standing by my side.
All:	Sardines!
Leader:	Every morning when I go to the store.
All:	Sardines!
Leader:	See the people there begging for more. I got sardines on my plate and I don't need no steak, with . . .
All:	Sardines!
Group:	Hey!

Leader:	And pork and beans!
Group:	Hey!
Leader:	Sardines on a Monday.
Group:	Hey! Hey!
Leader:	On a Tuesday and a Wednesday.
Group:	Hey! Hey!
Leader:	I got sardines on a Thursday.
Group:	Hey! Hey!
Leader:	On a Friday and a Saturday.
Group:	Hey! Hey!
Leader:	I got sardines on my plate and I don't need no steak, with . . .
All:	Sardines!
Group:	Hey!
Leader:	And pork and beans!
Group:	Hey!
All:	SARDINES!

Kids appreciate the humor in this snappy, quirky little ode to the sardine. They also love to shout, and in this call and response song, they have plenty of opportunity to do just that. Tell them, "Every time I do *this* (hold out both arms toward them) I want you to shout, 'Hey!'" Then practice doing it twice in quick succession for the "Hey! Hey!" so that they get the timing right. "Now when I do *this* (point fingers at them), shout 'Sardines!'"

Swing Low, Sweet Chariot

AUDIENCE:
Kindergarten through
sixth grade

TIME:
3 minutes

Swing low, sweet chariot,

comin' for to carry me home.

Swing low, sweet chariot,

comin' for to carry me home.

I looked over Jordan, and what did I see?

Comin' for to carry me home.

A band of angels comin' after me,

comin' for to carry me home.

Swing low, sweet chariot,

comin' for to carry me home.

Swing low, sweet chariot,

comin' for to carry me home.

It is so much fun to watch faces light up when you infuse new life into a classic! For this stretcher, let yourself go, especially when you get to the phrase "sweet chariot." It is easy to teach, because most people already know the words and the tune. Just tell your audience, "You already know this one. Just sing right along and do what I do!"

ACTIONS

Swing low, *(With fists holding invisible swing ropes, move front to back in swinging motion, while gradually lowering height by bending knees.)*

sweet chariot, *(Hold reins of invisible chariot, with body vibrating as if on bumpy road.)*

comin' *(Make beckoning signal.)*

for *(Hold up four fingers.)*

to *(Hold up two fingers.)*

carry *(Swing invisible sack over shoulder.)*

me *(Point to self.)*

home *(Hug self.)*

I *(Point to eye.)*

looked over Jordan, *(With hand shading eyes, peer out at audience.)*

and what *(Shrug and shake head in puzzlement.)*

did I *(Point to self.)*

see? *(Point outward from eyes with two index fingers.)*

A band *(Strum your air guitar.)*

of angels *(Look angelic and flutter your hands to indicate wings.)*

comin' *(Make beckoning sign.)*

after *(Glance over shoulder and point over shoulder with thumb.)*

me, *(Point to self.)*

comin' *(Make beckoning sign.)*

for *(Hold up four fingers.)*

to *(Hold up two fingers.)*

carry *(Swing invisible sack over shoulder.)*

me *(Point to self.)*

home *(Hug self.)*

Bill Grogan's Goat

Leader: There was a man.

Group: There was a man.

Leader: Now please take note.

Group: Now please take note.

Leader: There was a man

Group: There was a man

Leader: who had a goat.

Group: who had a goat.

Leader: He loved that goat,

Group: He loved that goat,

Leader: indeed he did.

Group: indeed he did.

Leader: He loved that goat

Group: He loved that goat

Leader: just like a kid.

Group: just like a kid.

Bill Grogan's goat
was feeling fine.
Ate three red shirts
from off the line.
Bill took a stick,
gave him a whack,
and tied that goat
to the railroad track.

The whistle blew.
The train drew nigh.
Bill Grogan's goat
was doomed to die.
He gave three coughs
of awful pain,
coughed up those shirts,
and flagged that train!

Bill Grogan's goat
got on that train,
then took a boat
to far-off Spain.
Now no one whacks
him with a stick.
He can eat red shirts
'til he gets sick.

This song is lively and humorous. Best of all, it is an echo song, which practically guarantees success. Simply ask your audience to be your echo and sing the song phrase by phrase. Your audience will echo it right back.

STORYTELLER'S TIP:
While attracted to the bouncy melody, clever wordplay and plot twists in this song, I was put off by the implications of abuse. In order to sing this song with a clear conscience, I had to write my own concluding verse, in which my goat goes on the lam and escapes his cruel owner.

I'll Tell My Ma

AUDIENCE:
Kindergarten
through
middle school

TIME:
3 minutes

I'll tell my ma when I go home,

the boys won't leave the girls alone.

They pull my hair, they stole my comb,

but that's all right 'til I go home.

She is handsome, she is pretty.

She's the belle of Belfast city.

She is courting, one, two, three.

Please can you tell me, who is he?

74

Albert Mooney says he loves her.

All the boys are fighting for her.

They knock on the door and they ring at the bell,

saying, "Oh, my true love, are you well?"

Out she comes as white as snow,

rings on her fingers and bells on her toes.

I tell you more, she says she'll die

if she doesn't get the fella with the roving eye.

Let the wind and the rain and the hail blow high,

and the snow come tumbling from the sky.

She's as nice as apple pie,

and she'll get her own lad by and by.

When she gets a lad of her own,

she won't tell her ma when she gets home.

Let them all come as they will,

it's Albert Mooney loves her still.

This is a traditional street rhyme from Ireland, and makes a lovely complement to a program of Irish stories. It also tells a very sweet, if bittersweet, love story. To add an element of audience participation, I ask the audience to learn a little eight-beat clapping game and to accompany me when I sing:

1. Slap thighs with hands.
2. Clap hands together.
3. Snap fingers with right hand.
4. Clap hands together.
5. Snap fingers with left hand.

STORYTELLER'S TIP:

Don't get too caught up in trying to make the clapping work out beat for beat. It doesn't really matter, and the audience won't know the difference. It always ends on the right note for me, and here is the trick I use: When I approach the last line, wherever I am in the clapping sequence, I slow down my song, and conclude . . .

It's Albert Mooney *(Snap or clap, wherever you are in the sequence.)* loves *(Clap.)* her *(Clap).* still. *(Clap.)*

6. Clap hands together.

7. Snap fingers on both right and left hands.

8. Clap hands together.

First teach the clapping sequence to your audience, starting slowly, and then speed it up as they learn. Then add the music, reassuring them that they will pick it up as they go. When using this game with the song, it will go roughly like this:

I'll (*Slap thighs with hands.*)

tell (*Clap hands together.*)

my (*Snap fingers with right hand.*)

ma (*Clap hands together.*)

when (*Snap fingers with left hand.*)

I (*Clap both hands together.*)

go (*Snap right and left fingers simultaneously.*)

home (*Clap hands together.*),

the (*Slap thighs with both hands.*)

boys (*Clap hands together.*)

won't (*Snap right fingers.*)

leave (*Clap hands together.*)

the (*Snap left fingers.*)

girls (*Clap hands together.*)

alone. (*Snap right and left fingers simultaneously.*)

Little Cabin in the Forest Green

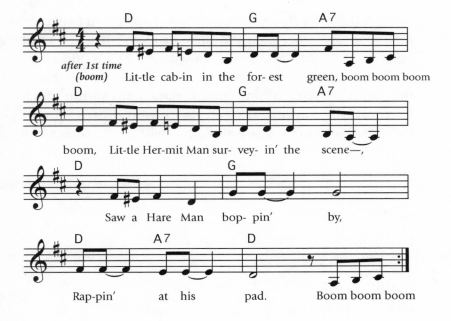

AUDIENCE:
Kindergarten through sixth grade

TIME:
6 minutes

Little cabin in the forest green.
Boom, boom, boom, boom!
Little Hermit Man surveyin' the scene
saw a Hare Man boppin' by,
rappin' at his pad.
Boom, boom, boom, boom!

"Like, help! Like, help!" came the plea.
Boom, boom, boom, boom!
"Agriculture Man exterminate me!"
"Come on, Hare Man, come with me,
safely you will always be."
Boom, boom, boom, boom!

Kids will always prefer this jazzed-up version to its more traditional predecessor, "Little Cabin in the Woods." The first time through, sing the entire song with all the hand motions. The next time through, don't sing the first line but continue making the motions. The next time through, don't sing the first or second line. Each time you drop another line until you're acting out the entire song with no words and using just hand motions. The challenge, however, is to keep singing the "Boom, boom, boom, boom." Don't spend too much time teaching this one. You can assure your audience truthfully, "If you don't know it now, you will by the time we're finished!"

ACTIONS

Little cabin in the forest green. (*Trace a cabin with index fingers.*)

Boom, boom, boom, boom!

Little Hermit Man surveyin' the scene (*Place hand over eye and peer in all directions.*)

saw a Hare Man boppin' by, (*Hold up two fingers of one hand to make rabbit ears hopping by.*)

rappin' at his pad. (*Knock on imaginary door with fist.*)

Boom, boom, boom, boom!

"Like, help! Like, help!" came the plea. (*Fling hands back to shoulder level on "help!"*)

"Agriculture Man exterminate me!" (*Make a choppy pointing motion, alternating right and left forefingers.*)

"Come on, Hare Man, come with me, (*Make a beckoning motion.*)

safely you will always be." (*Make bunny ears with one hand; stroke them gently with the other.*)

Boom, boom, boom, boom!

STORYTELLER'S TIP:

As the song goes on and your audience is catching on, pick up the pace. I mouth the silent words and use exaggerated hand motions begun a fraction of an instant early, so that the audience can anticipate its parts, even the silent ones.

Hi-Ho-Jerum

AUDIENCE:
First through
sixth grades

TIME:
4 minutes

There was a rich man and he lived in Jerusalem.

Glory hallelujah, hi-ho-jerum.

He wore a silk hat and he dressed very sprucium.

Glory hallelujah, hi-ho-jerum.

CHORUS

Hi-ho-jerum. Hi-ho-jerum.
Skinnamarink-a-doodlium.
Skinnamarink-a-doodlium.
Glory hallelujah, hi-ho-jerum.

To his gate came a human wreckium.
Glory hallelujah, hi-ho-jerum.
He wore a bowler with the rim around his neckium.
Glory hallelujah, hi-ho-jerum.

The poor man asked for a piece of bread and cheesium.
Glory hallelujah, hi-ho-jerum.
The rich man said, "I'm going to call the policium."
Glory hallelujah, hi-ho-jerum.

The poor man died and his soul went to heavium.
Glory hallelujah, hi-ho-jerum.
He danced with the angels 'til a quarter past elevium.
Glory hallelujah, hi-ho-jerum.

The rich man died, but he didn't fare so wellium.
Glory hallelujah, hi-ho-jerum.
He couldn't go to heaven, so he had to go belowium.
Glory hallelujah, hi-ho-jerum.

The devil said, 'This is no hotelium."
Glory hallelujah, hi-ho-jerum.
"So get to work and start shoveling coalium."
Glory hallelujah hi-ho-jerum.

The moral of this story is that riches are no jokium.

Glory hallelujah, hi-ho-jerum.

We'll all go to heaven, 'cause we're all stoney brokium.

Glory hallelujah, hi-ho-jerum.

The verses of this song are clever bits of wordplay, the chorus is cheerful and bouncy, and the ending of this story satisfies. Invite your audience to join in on the second and fourth lines of each verse, *"Glory hallelujah, hi-ho-jerum,"* as well as on the chorus in between verses. They will jump right inium.

Pirate Ship

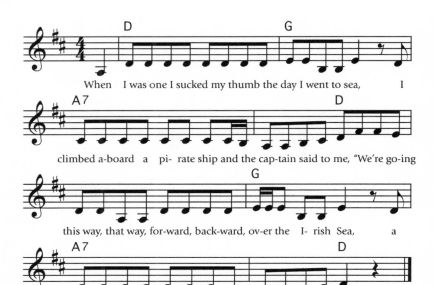

When I was one I sucked my thumb the day I went to sea, I climbed a-board a pi- rate ship and the cap-tain said to me, "We're go-ing this way, that way, for-ward, back-ward, ov-er the I- rish Sea, a Dra-ma-mine when I turn green and that's the life for me.

When I was one, *(Hold up one finger.)*

I sucked my thumb. *(Pretend to suck thumb.)*

The day I went to sea, *(Make waves with hand.)*

I climbed aboard a pirate ship, *(Climb an invisible ladder.)*

and the captain *(salute)* said to me,

"We're going this way, *(Jump right.)*

that way, *(Jump left.)*

forward, *(Jump forward.)*

backward, *(Jump backward.)*

over the Irish Sea." *(Make waves with hand.)*

A Dramamine *(Pop a pill in mouth.)*

when I turn green, *(Hold tummy and look sick.)*

and that's *(Hold out arms.)*

the life *(Double thumbs up.)*

for me! *(Point thumbs at chest.)*

Pirates will always be a hit with kids. This song has plenty of action and a catchy chorus. If you are working with a group on a regular basis, you can also have children volunteer their own ideas for verses. "When I was three, I learned to ski . . ."

OTHER VERSES

When I was two: stepped in goo. *(Lift shoe and shake.)*

Three: scratched my flea. *(Scratch.)*

Four: shut the door. *(Shut an imaginary door.)*

Five: slapped some jive. *(Do a little dance.)*

Six: picked up sticks. *(Pick up invisible sticks.)*

Seven: went to heaven. *(Point upward and act "angelic.")*

Eight: shut the gate. *(Pretend to shut gate.)*

Nine: stood in line. *(Tap foot and look at watch.)*

Ten: did it again. *(Shrug.)*

Ravioli!

AUDIENCE:
Kindergarten through sixth grade

TIME:
5 minutes or more, depending on the number of verses and the degree of participation

CHORUS

Ravioli, we love ravioli.

Ravioli, that's the stuff for me!

Leader: Do you have it on your sleeve?

Group: Yes, I have it on my sleeve.

Leader: On your sleeve?

Group: On my sleeve.

All: Oooooooooh!

CHORUS

Ravioli, we love ravioli.

Ravioli, that's the stuff for me!

Leader: Do you have it on your pants?

Group: Yes, I have it on my pants.

Leader: On your pants?

Group: On my pants.

Leader: On your sleeve?

Group: On my sleeve.

All: Oooooooooh!

CHORUS

Ravioli, we love ravioli.

Ravioli, that's the stuff for me!

Leader: Do you have it on your shoe?

Group: Yes, I have it on my shoe.

Leader: On your shoe?

Group: On my shoe.

Leader: On your pants?

Group: On my pants.

Leader: On your sleeve?

Group: On my sleeve.

All: Oooooooh. . . .

STORYTELLER'S TIP:

This is a great stretcher to pair with "On Top of Spaghetti," found in my book, Crazy Gibberish, or with Tomi DePaoli's Strega Nona and the Magic Pasta Pot.

I enjoy the playful interaction in this cumulative song, sung to the tune of "Alouette." Singers can add as many articles of clothing or body parts as they can think of: chin, hair, socks, shoes, collar, tie, bib, even pajamas! There is more than one way to involve the audience, depending on time constraints, setting, and the degree of formality a group leader wishes to maintain. Once I have established the call and response pattern between the leader and the group, I sometimes invite children to raise their hands and volunteer ideas for the next verse. Just ask them to wait to raise their hands until you stop singing after each verse, or some children will be waving their hands to be called upon throughout the entire song.

You can also have the volunteers come up to the front of the room one at a time, at the end of each verse, to share their suggestions. Each new volunteer should take her place at the end of the line and maintain that place throughout subsequent verses. When you sing out the long list of garments, you need only walk down the line behind the volunteers and have each one, in turn, sing and point. You might want to limit this song to eight or nine verses. It is better to leave your audience members wanting more than to have them lose interest. You can speed it up as the group becomes familiar with the words and tune.

ACTIONS

Have singers point to each garment as they sing out its name.

The Little Green Frog

AUDIENCE:
Preschool
through
fifth grade.

TIME:
2 minutes

MMM-mmm went the little green frog one day.

MMM-mmm went the little green frog.

MMM-mmm went the little green frog one day.

And they all went MMM-mmm-ah!

We all know frogs go . . .

(*Clap!*) Lah-dee-dah-dee-dah.

(*Clap!*) Lah-dee-dah-dee-dah.

(*Clap!*) Lah-dee-dah-dee-dah.

We all know frogs go . . .

(*Clap!*) Lah-dee-dah-dee-dah.

They don't go MMM-mmm-ah!

This song is surprisingly challenging, and it takes practice not to "*MMM*" when you want to "*mmm.*" That might explain the appeal that it holds for such a wide range of ages, or perhaps we all just need an excuse to stick out our tongues now and then. Sing the first part of the song, then give your audience no more than half a minute to practice before singing it all together. The clapping is so easy that you don't even have to teach it. Just cruise from the first part into the lah-dee-dahs, and the audience will follow.

ACTIONS

MMM (*Shut eyes and press lips together while making humming sound.*)

mmm (*Open eyes and stick out tongue while making humming sound.*)

ah (*Open mouth and eyes while singing "ah."*)

We all know frogs go

(*Clap!*) Lah-dee-dah-dee-dah. (*Flutter right hand high and left hand low.*)

(*Clap!*) Lah-dee-dah-dee-dah. (*Switch and flutter left hand high and right hand low.*)

(*Clap!*) Lah-dee-dah-dee-dah. (*Switch back to fluttering right hand high, left low.*)

We all know frogs go

(*Clap!*) Lah-dee-dah-dee-dah. (*Switch back to fluttering left hand high, right low.*)

They don't go MMM (*Shut eyes and lips together making humming sound.*)

mmm (*Open eyes and stick out tongue while making humming sound.*)

ah! (*Open mouth and eyes while singing "ah."*)

Mrs. Murphy's Chowder

AUDIENCE:
Third grade
through adult

TIME:
5 minutes,
including time
to teach the
chorus

Won't you bring back, won't you bring back Mrs. Murphy's chowder?

It was tuneful, every spoonful made you yodel louder.

After dinner Uncle Ben used to fill his fountain pen

from a plate of Mrs. Murphy's chowder.

CHORUS

It had ice cream, cold cream, benzine, gasoline,

soup beans, string beans, floating all around.

Sponge cake, beefsteak, mistake, stomachache,

cream puffs, earmuffs, many to be found.

Silk hats, doormats, bed slats, democrats,

cowbells, doorbells beckon you to dine.

Meatballs, fish balls, mothballs, cannonballs;

come on in, the chowder's fine.

Won't you bring back, won't you bring back Mrs. Murphy's chowder?

With each helping, you'll be yelping for a headache powder.

And if you dig in very far, you might find a motor car

in a plate of Mrs. Murphy's chowder.

CHORUS

Won't you bring back, won't you bring back Mrs. Murphy's chowder?

You can pack it, you can stack it all around the larder.

The plumber died the other day; they embalmed him right away,

with a plate of Mrs. Murphy's chowder.

CHORUS

This delicious chorus is challenging even for older audiences, but that, along with its slightly irreverent tone, is what appeals to teenagers. I would not introduce this to an audience in a performance situation and expect them to master it in one session. However, it is perfect for summer camp and is a favorite with my Junior Girl Scouts, who can sing it backwards and forwards and in their sleep.

STORYTELLER'S TIP:
Try singing the verses at a dignified pace; then sing the tongue-twisting chorus as fast as you can. The contrast is very funny. This also works as a humorous musical skit. Kids can make props and act it out as they sing.

Purple Lights

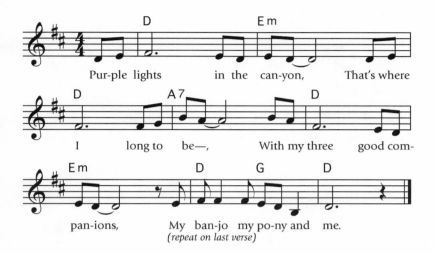

AUDIENCE:
Second grade
through adult

TIME:
2 minutes

Leader: Purple lights

Group: Purple lights

Leader: in the canyon.

Group: in the canyon.

Leader: That's where I

Group: That's where I

Leader: long to be.

Group: long to be.

Leader: with my three

Group: with my three

Leader: good companions.

Group: good companions,

All: My banjo, my pony, and me.

Whippoorwill . . . in the willow

Sings a sweet . . . melody

STORYTELLER'S TIP:

If you hang onto the
last note of each phrase
for an instant after your
audience chimes in, there
is a blending of voices that
creates a lovely effect.

For my three . . . good companions,

My banjo, my pony, and me.

No more goats . . . to be ropin.'

No more stray . . . will I see.

Just my three . . . good companions,

my banjo, my pony, and me.

This song is perfect for singing around a campfire and is also great for closing a program; people go home feeling mellow. It is an echo song, with the leader singing each phrase echoed by the audience, with one exception. Tell the group, "You be my echo, except for the last line of each verse, which we will sing together. It's easy; just one line to learn." Sing it for them, sing it once together, and then begin. When you get to the last line, cue your audience with a nod of the head and a lifted hand.

Mmmm, I Want to Linger

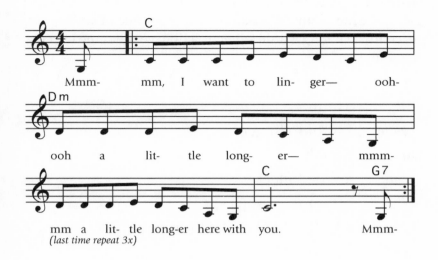

Mmm- mm, I want to lin- ger— ooh-

ooh a lit- tle long- er— mmm-

mm a lit- tle long-er here with you. Mmm-
(last time repeat 3x)

AUDIENCE:
Third grade
through adult

TIME:
2 minutes

Mmmm, I want to linger,
ooooh, a little longer,
mmmm, a little longer here with you.

Mmmm, it's such a perfect night,
ooooh, it doesn't seem quite right,
mmmm, that this is my last night with you.

Mmmm, and come September,
ooooh, I will remember,
mmmm, those special days I shared with you.

Mmmm, and as the years go by,
ooooh, I'll think of you and sigh.
Mmmm, this is goodnight and not goodbye.

    This sweet song is the perfect way to conclude a conference, a workshop, a camp session, a school year, or even a very special performance. The leader can invite people to chime in on

the Mmmms and Oooohs. Once you start singing this song, your group will very likely want to linger a little longer, so when you get to the end, sing it through one more time. The second time around, repeat the last line three or four times, each time singing a little softer. It will have the same effect as a group hug.

All: Mmmm,
Leader: I want to linger,
All: ooooh,
Leader: a little longer,
All: mmmm,
Leader: a little longer here with you.

All: Mmmm,
Leader: it's such a perfect night,
All: ooooh,
Leader: it doesn't seem quite right,
All: mmmm,
Leader: that this is my last night with you.

All: Mmmm,
Leader: and come September,
All: ooooh,
Leader: I will remember,
All: mmmm,
Leader: those special days I shared with you.

All: Mmmm,
Leader: and as the years go by,
All: ooooh,
Leader: I'll think of you and sigh.
All: Mmmm,
Leader: this is goodnight and not goodbye.

STORYTELLER'S TIP:
To help your audience anticipate its part, point out that each verse has three lines, and if they put the first letter of each line together, they spell "M-O-M." When using this stretcher, you can substitute "those special days" with camping, Scouting, or school days, depending on the group.

May There Always Be Sunshine

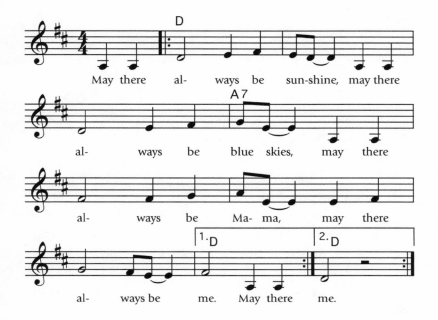

AUDIENCE:
Preschool
through adult

TIME:
2 minutes

May there always be sunshine.
May there always be blue skies.
May there always be Mama.
May there always be me.

May there always be sunshine.
May there always be blue skies.
May there always be Mama.
May there always be me.

IN RUSSIAN

Poost vsyegda boodyet solntzye.
Poost vsyegda boodyet nyeba.
Poost vsyegda boodyet Mama.
Poost vsyegda boodoo ya.

Poost vsyegda boodyet solntzye.

Poost vsyegda boodyet nyeba.

Poost vsyegda boodyet Mama.

Poost vsyegda boodoo ya.

This gentle song was written by a Russian schoolchild. When introducing it, I ask the audience to sing along with their hands, and I accompany myself with American Sign Language. I often sing it first in Russian, with the children following along with ASL. When the children hear this song in both English and ASL, a light goes on in their eyes as they connect the words they are singing with the words they are signing. It is an important song that illustrates how humanity's most basic values are shared everywhere. It is also empowering for children to know that one child's voice can indeed be heard all around the world.

Keep Breathing

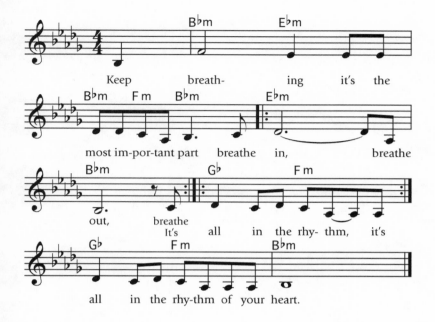

AUDIENCE:
Kindergarten
through adult

TIME:
3 minutes

Keep breathing; it's the most important part.

Breathe in, breathe out. Breathe in, breathe out.

Breathe in, breathe out. Breathe in, breathe out.

It's all in the rhythm, it's all in the rhythm.

It's all in the rhythm of your heart.

Some story stretchers are made to raise the energy level of an audience. This gentle song will soothe your group and slow it down. Sing it through several times, just for the pleasure of it. As my friend Kaaren Moitoza says, "It is a wonderful way to get a roomful of people all into the same heartspace."

Knee Slappers, Rib Ticklers, and Tongue Twisters

Knock-Knock

Knock-knock.

Who's there?

Colleen.

Colleen who?

Colleen all cars, we have a knock-knock joke in progress!

Like baseball, jazz, and Elvis, knock-knock jokes are a phenomenon deeply and uniquely rooted in American history, and they are here to stay. Listed below are some knock-knock jokes that would easily fit into a storytelling program. Some were chosen because they relate in some way to storytelling, or have been adapted to do so. Many play upon familiar fairy tales, while others could be used to introduce a particular story or stretcher. They are the ideal way to make a transition between stories, as they instantly and effectively engage audience members, who are already conditioned to respond. Just call out, "Knock-knock!" and they will not only reply, "Who's there?," but will wait in eager and automatic anticipation for your answer!

Knock-knock.

Who's there?

Paul.

Paul who?

Paul up a chair and I'll tell you a story.

Knock-knock.

Who's there?

Lena

Lena who?

Lena little closer, so I don't have to yell.

Knock-knock.
Who's there?
Howie.
Howie who?
Howie 'bout another story?

Knock-knock.
Who's there?
Avenue.
Avenue who?
Avenue heard that story before?

Knock-knock.
Who's there?
Foyer.
Foyer who?
Foyer information, it's the big bad wolf!

Knock-knock.
Who's there?
Hugh.
Hugh who?
Hugh's afraid of the big bad wolf?

Knock-knock.
Who's there?
Midas.
Midas who?
Midas well open the door; I'm not going away.

Knock-knock.
Who's there?
Bella.
Bella who?
Bella the ball.

Knock-knock.
Who's there?
Ooze.
Ooze who?
Ooze that walking on my bridge?

Knock-knock.
Who's there?
Booty.
Booty who?
Booty and the Beast.

Knock-knock.
Who's there?
Farrah.
Farrah who?
Farrah tales *can* come true.

Knock-knock.
Who's there?
Andy.
Andy who?
Andy all lived happily ever after.

Knock-knock.
Who's there?
Shelby.
Shelby who?
Shelby be comin' round the mountain.

Knock-knock.
Who's there?
Bea.
Bea who?
Bea afraid . . . be very afraid!

Knock-knock.
Who's there?
Nadia.
Nadia who?
Nadia believe me?

Knock-knock.
Who's there?
Ben and Don.
Ben and Don who?
Ben there, Don that.

Knock-knock.
Who's there?
Colonel.
Colonel who?
Colonel of truth.

Knock-knock.
Who's there?
Dexter.
Dexter who?
Dexter halls with boughs of holly.

Knock-knock.
Who's there?
Tom Sawyer.
Tom Sawyer who?
Tom Sawyer paint job on his fence, and, boy, are you in trouble!

Knock-knock.
Who's there?
Venue.
Venue who?
Venue vish upon a star.

Knock-knock.
Who's there?
Salada.
Salada who?
Salada bad knock-knock jokes going around.

Knock-knock.
Who's there?
Otto.
Otto who?
Otto be a law against all these knock-knock jokes!

Knock-knock.

Who's there?

Anita.

Anita who?

Anita another knock-knock joke like Anita hole
in the head.

Knock-knock.

Who's there?

Wystan.

Wystan who?

Wystan civilization is in trouble if it can't produce
anything more profound than knock-knock jokes.

Knock-knock.

Who's there?

Althea.

Althea who?

Althea later, alligator.

Knock-knock.

Who's there?

Thistle.

Thistle who?

Thistle be the last knock-knock joke, I promise!

American Riddles

Q. What did the first little pig say after the wolf blew down his house?

A. "That's the last straw!"

Q. Why did the three little pigs leave home?

A. Because their father was an awful boar.

Q. How did the tortoise do in his famous race?

A. He won by a hare.

Q. What do you get when you cross Cinderella's footman with the Frog Prince?

A. Foot Prince.

Q. Who is beautiful and gray and wears glass slippers?

A. Cinderelephant.

Q. What's gray, has large wings, a long nose, and gives money to elephants?

A. The Tusk Fairy.

Q. Why didn't the princess sleep well on top of twenty mattresses?

A. Would you sleep well if you could fall that far out of bed?

Q. What do dragons do on their birthdays?

A. They light their candles, and the cake, and the presents . . .

Q. What do dragons eat with their soup?

A. Firecrackers.

Q. What do you get if you cross a mosquito with a knight?

A. A bite in shining armor.

Q. What does a near-sighted gingerbread man use for eyes?

A. Contact raisins.

Q. How does a broom tell stories?

A. With sweeping gestures.

Q. How does a hot dog tell stories?

A. Frankly.

Q. Why don't shoes tell stories?

A. Because they are either tongue-tied or have a foot in their mouth.

Q. When is the best time to tell ghost stories?

A. When the spirits move you.

Q. Why can't you tell stories about a bed?

A. Because it hasn't been made up yet.

Q. Why does an elephant have cracks between his toes?

A. To carry his library card.

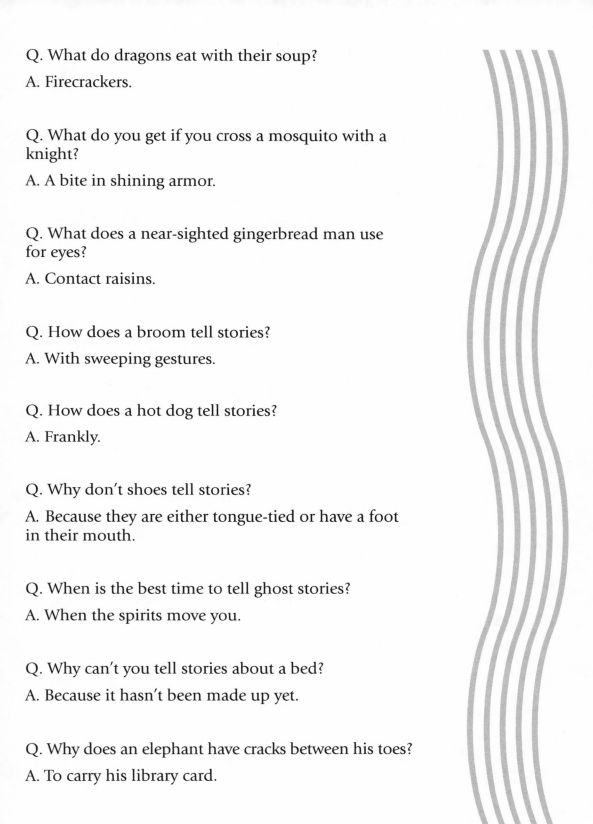

Q. Why did the librarian slip and fall?

A. She was in the nonfriction section.

Q. Why should you never tell a secret near the clock?

A. Because time will tell.

Q. Why did the reporter shine a flashlight into his mouth?

A. Because he wanted to get the inside story.

Q. What does it mean when you find a horseshoe?

A. It means that somewhere a horse is going barefoot.

Q. What happens when you cross poison ivy with a four-leaf clover?

A. You get a rash of good luck!

Q. What's orange and keeps falling off walls?

A. Humpty Pumpkin.

Q. Could Humpty Dumpty have survived his fall?

A. If so, he would have been only a shell of his former self.

Q. What goes, "Ho, ho, ho, plop?"

A. Santa Claus laughing his head off.

Q. Where does the Sandman keep his sleeping sand?

A. In his nap sack.

Q. What did Dr. Frankenstein get when he put his dog's brain in the body of a fish?

A. I don't know, but it loves to chase submarines.

Q. When you see three monsters wearing pink jackets, what does that tell you?

A. That they're on the same team.

Q. What do you get when you cross a centipede with a chicken?

A. I'm not sure, but everybody gets a drumstick.

Q. What's gray on the inside and clear on the outside?

A. An elephant in a baggie.

Q. What made Francis Scott Key famous?

A. He actually knew all the verses to the "Star-Spangled Banner."

Q. Did you hear the story about the jump rope?

A. Skip it.

Q. Did you hear the story about the germ?

A. Never mind, I don't want it spread around.

Q. Did you hear the story about the peacock?

A. It's a beautiful tale.

Q. Did you hear the story about the roof?

A. Never mind, it's over your head.

Q. Did you hear the story about the skunk?

A. Never mind, it stinks.

Q. Did you hear the story about the burp?

A. Never mind, it's not worth repeating.

Traditional Riddles from Many Lands

Q. How far is it from the surface of the ocean to its greatest depth?

A. A stone's throw. (France)

Q. What has no tongue, but talks of everything?

A. A book. (Siberia)

Q. What is with you from the day you crawl to the day you die, yet during storms, it deserts you?

A. Your shadow. (Hawaii)

Q. It's a bottomless barrel, shaped like a hive, full of flesh, and the flesh is alive.

A. A sewing thimble. (Ireland)

Q. How many sides does a bagel have?

A. Two, one inside and one outside. (Jewish)

Q. What is as old as the mountains?

A. The valleys between them. (Wales)

Q. Rita, Rita shouts in the forest, and at home she is silent.

A. The ax. (Argentina)

Q. A hill full, a hole full, ye cannot catch a bowl full. What is it?

A. The mist. (Scotland)

Q. The more you take from it in front, the more you add on to it behind. What is it?

A. The road you travel. (Italy)

Q. When does a duck start swimming?

A. When its feet no longer touch the bottom. (Estonia)

Q. Wind wrapped in paper. What is it?

A. A fan. (China)

Q. What is it that everyone would like, but when they get it, they don't like it?

A. Old age. (Jewish)

Q. Who can take a thousand people to town in one small wagon?

A. Anyone willing to make enough trips. (Denmark)

Q. What travels faster than anything?

A. Your thoughts. (Arapaho)

Q. What comes walking on four feet and has a tiled roof?

A. A turtle. (Thailand)

Q. Who can boast of the greatest deeds in the world?

A. A braggart. (Germany)

Q. Riddle me, riddle me, what is that that is over the head and beneath the hat?

A. Hair. (England)

Q. A handful of rice scattered on a blue cloth?

A. The sky and the stars. (India)

Q. Two sisters: one knows everything, and the other knows nothing. Who are they?

A. Right and left hands. (Spain)

Q. Why does the stork stand on one leg?

A. Because if it lifted the other one up it would fall down. (Egypt)

Q. What can be broken by the softest of whispers?

A. Silence. (Puerto Rico)

Q. An old bald man keeps chasing five little brothers, but he never catches up with them. Who are they?

A. The heel and toes of a foot. (Finland)

Q. My house has no door, and if it should break, no one can fix it. What am I?

A. An egg. (Africa: Swahili)

Q. Why does a watch always stop when it falls on the floor?

A. Because it can't go through the floor. (Cuba)

Q. I go running, and when I arrive, I bend down and let my white hairs fall forward. Who am I?

A. A wave. (Philippines)

Q. What is it that you look at with one eye, but never with two?

A. The inside of a bottle. (Africa: Ga)

Q. We have two legs, but can go nowhere without a man, and he can go nowhere without us. Who are we?

A. Trousers. (Spain)

Q. A small house with two windows opened at morning and closed at night. What is it?

A. A pair of eyes. (Hungary)

Q. In the beginning I seem mysterious, but in the end I am nothing serious. What am I?

A. A riddle. (United States)

Tongue Twisters and Tanglers

Q: What is a tongue twister?

A: It's when your tang gets all tongled up!

I'm not sure why people enjoy tripping on their tongues, but they do, and it seems that they always have. Peter Piper was already picking his pack of pickled peppers back in 1674, when that tongue twister was first published in an English grammar book.

Tongue twisters have many practical uses. Actors and professional speakers, including storytellers, use them as training exercises. As a group leader, your object can simply be to lead your audience in some fun.

If you want to show off a little, begin with a lively recitation of "Prinderella and the Since." Follow it with a challenge to your audience, tossing out a tongue twister and asking them to repeat it. Start with easier ones and work your way up to the more difficult ones. But remember to use tongue twisters sparingly, so as not to frustrate the less nimble-tongued. There will be plenty of giggles as they test their skills.

Say each of these phrases as fast as you can, ten times in a row!

A knapsack strap!

Norse myths!

Peggy Babcock!

A regal rural ruler!

Ape cakes!

Gig-whip!

Shining soldiers!

Chief sheep section!

Try saying each of these phrases as fast as you can, three times in a row!

Three blind mice blew bugles!

Slim Sam slid sideways!

Rush the washing, Russell!

Many an anemone sees an enemy anemone!

Sister Susie's sewing shirts for soldiers!

Four fat friars frying flat fish!

One cute king's kite caught quite quick!

A cup of proper coffee in a copper coffee pot!

A peck of pesky pixies!

Mrs. Smith's Fish Sauce Shop!

Prinderella and the Since

Here, indeed, is a story that will make your *cresh fleep*. It will give you *poose gimples*. Think of a poor little *glip of a surl, prairie vitty*, who, just because she had two *sisty uglers*, had to *flop the moard, cindel the shuvvers* out of the *pireflace*, and do all the other *chasty nores* while her *soamly histers* went to a *drancy bess fall*. Wasn't that a *shirty dame?*

Well, to make a long *shorry stort*, this *youngless hapster* was *chewing her doors* one day when who should suddenly appear but a *garry fawdmother. Beeling very fad* for this *witty prafe*, she *happed her clands*, said a couple of *wagic merds*, and *da ta!*

In the *ash of a flybrow*, the *gritty pearl* was transformed into a *bavaging reauty*. Out at the *sturbcone* stood a *nagmificent colden goach*, made of a *pipe rellow yumpkin*. The *gaudy fairmother* told her to hop in and *dive to the drance*, but added that she *must mositively* be *mid by homenight*. So, *overmoach with eecumtion*, she *fanked the tharry* from the *hottom of her bart, bimed acloard*, the driver *whacked his crip*, and off they went in a *dowd of clust*.

Soon they came to a *casterful wundel* where a *pransome hince* was *possing a tarty* for the *teeple of the pown. Kinderella alighted from the soach* and *hanked her dropperchief*. Out ran the *hinsome prance*, who had been peeking at her all the time from a *widden hindow*. The *sugly issters stood bylently sigh*, not *sinderizing Reckognella* in her *goyal rarments*.

Well, to make a long *shorry stort*, the *nince went absolutely pruts* over the *pruvvly lincess*. After *dowers of antsing*, he was *ayzier than crevver* about her. But at the *noke of stridmight, Scramderella suddenly sinned*, and the *aprinted poince dike to lied!* He had forgotten to ask the *nincess her prame!* But as she went *stunning*

AUDIENCE:
Third grade through adult

TIME:
3 minutes

STORYTELLER'S TIP:

You can be dramatic, but tell this one with a straight face. Don't rush your delivery, so that the audience can relish the wordplay.

down the long reps, she *slicked off one of the glass kippers* she was wearing, and the *pounce princed* upon it with *eeming glize.*

The next day he *tied all over trown* to find the *lainty daydy* whose foot *slitted that fipper.* And the *ditty prame* with the only *fit that footed* was none other than our *layding leedy.* So she finally *prairied the mince,* and they *happed livily after ever.*

This clever story is popular with adults as well as with children. Don't be intimidated by the language. At first glance, it might look like chaos, but there is actually method to the madness. Read the story aloud several times: it actually flows well, once you are familiar with the storyline. The story is so simple that only the italicized phrases require much attention. Once you internalize their original meaning, it is simply a matter of remembering to transpose a few letters until it becomes automatic. It will be well worth the effort to be able to pull this sure-fire crowd pleaser out of your bag of tricks.

The Limerick Song

AUDIENCE:
Second through sixth grades

TIME:
4 minutes

A canner exceedingly canny,

one morning remarked to his granny,

"A canner can can anything that he can,

but a canner can't can a can, can he?"

CHORUS

Aye-aye-aye-aye.

In Chile they never grow chilly.

So sing me another verse that's worse than the first.

Make sure that it's foolish and silly.

A tutor who tooted a flute

tried to tutor two tooters to toot.

Said the two to the tutor, "Is it tougher to toot

or to tutor two tooters to toot?"

A certain young fellow named Beebee

wished to marry a lady named Phoebe.

"But," said he, "I must see what the minister's fee be,

before Phoebe be Phoebe Beebee."

A flea and a fly in a flue

were caught, so what could they do?

Said the fly, "Let us flee." "Let us fly," said the flea.

So they flew through a flaw in the flue.

A lively young fisher named Fischer

used to fish from the edge of a fissure.

A fish with a grin pulled the fisherman in.

Now they're fishing the fissure for Fischer.

STORYTELLER'S TIP:

As with many stretchers, you can sing this or, if you prefer not to sing, chant it. Any limerick will work with this song, so keep your eyes and ears open for challenging limericks to add on to these verses. (I found the limerick about the flea and the fly in a joke book, and discovered the last verse about Fischer in an anthology of American folklore.) Another way to use this story stretcher is to have people volunteer to recite their favorite limerick, and have the whole group sing the chorus in between.

This song poses the sort of test that kids, especially those in the upper elementary grades, will enjoy. Begin by reciting the first verse as a spoken tongue twister. Then have them echo it back to you two lines at a time. Put it all together, then bring it up to tempo. Now you can tell them that they have actually learned the first verse to a tongue twister of a song. Sing the chorus, sing the first verse, and teach them the second verse in the same manner. Run through the chorus again as a bridge to the third verse.

Tree Toad Trials

AUDIENCE:
Third grade
through adult

TIME:
3 minutes

A tree toad loved a she-toad

that lived up in a tree.

She was a three-toed tree toad,

but a two-toed toad was he.

The two-toed toad tried to win

the she-toad's friendly nod,

for the two-toed toad loved the ground

on which the three-toed toad trod.

But no matter how the two-toed toad tried,

he could not please her whim.

In her tree-toad bower,

with her three-toed power,

the she-toad vetoed him.

    This tongue twister actually tells a story. So your audience can appreciate the story line, enunciate clearly and do not rush your delivery. This twister also can be performed a line at a time with the audience acting as your echo. But if you do it as an echo piece, first give a proper solo recitation of this poem, which the audience will bear in mind even as you break it into smaller bites.

ACTIONS

A tree toad loved a she-toad (*Pat hair into place with right hand showing three extended fingers and flutter eyelids.*)

that lived up in a tree. (*Point up and look up to where finger is pointing.*)

She was a three-toed tree toad, (*Show right hand with three fingers held up.*)

but a two-toed toad was he. (*Show left hand with two fingers held up and nod earnestly.*)

The two-toed toad tried to win (*Hold up left hand with two fingers.*)

the she-toad's friendly nod, (*Smile and give an exaggerated wink.*)

for the two-toed toad (*Hold up left and with two fingers.*)

loved the ground (*Clutch both hands to heart.*)

on which the three-toed toad trod. (*Hold up right hand with three fingers, then point to floor.*)

But no matter how (*Shrug and shake head in puzzlement.*)

the two-toed toad tried, (*Hold up left hand with two fingers.*)

he could not please her whim. (*Shake head and sigh deeply.*)

In her tree-toad bower, (*Point up.*)

with her three-toed power, (*Hold up right hand with three fingers.*)

the she-toad (*Pat hair into place with three fingers extended on right hand.*)

vetoed him. (*Give a double thumbs down.*)

STORYTELLER'S TIP:

To help your audience distinguish the three-toed she-toad from the two-toed he-toad, I have created simple, but distinct, hand signs to represent each character. This will help the audience visualize the frogs and know right away which one I am referring to. To keep myself from getting confused, I represent the female three-toed toad with my right hand and three fingers, as that is also the hand and the sign Girl Scouts use when saying their promise.

IF YOU WANT TO DIG DEEPER:
A BIBLIOGRAPHY OF RESOURCES

BOOKS

Baltuck, Naomi. *Crazy Gibberish and Other Story Hour Stretches.* Hamden, Conn.: Linnet Books, 1993.

Beall, Pamela Conn, and Susan Hagen Nipp. *Wee Sing Silly Songs.* Los Angeles: Price Stern Sloan, 1982.

Brandreth, Gyles. *The Biggest Tongue Twister Book in the World.* New York: Sterling Publishing Company, 1978.

Brown, Marc. *Finger Rhymes.* New York: E.P. Dutton, 1980.

_____. *Hand Rhymes.* New York: E.P. Dutton, 1985.

Carlson, Bernice Wells. *Listen! And Help Tell the Story.* Nashville, Tenn.: Abingdon Press, 1965.

Cobb, Jane. *I'm a Little Teapot: Presenting Preschool Storytime.* Vancouver: Black Sheep Press, 2001.

Cole, Joanna, and Stephanie Calmenso. *The Eentsy, Weentsy Spider: Fingerplays and Action Ryhmes.* New York: Mulberry Books, 1991.

Currie, Mary. *The Singing Sack.* London: A&C Black, 1989.

Delamar, Gloria T. *Children's Counting-Out Rhymes, Fingerplays, Jump-Rope and Ball-Bounce Chants, and Other Rhymes.* Jefferson, N.C.: McFarland, 1983.

Dundas, Marjorie. *Riddling Tales from Around the World.* Jackson, Miss.: University of Mississippi Press, 2002.

Flint Public Library. *Ring a Ring o' Roses: Finger Plays for Preschool Children.* Flint, Mich.: Flint Board of Education, 1996.

Fowke, Edith. *Sally Go Round the Sun: 300 Songs, Rhymes, and Games of Canadian Children.* Toronto: McClelland and Steward, 1969.

Glazer, Tom. *Do Your Ears Hang Low? Fifty More Musical Fingerplays.* New York: Doubleday, 1980.

_____. *Eye Winker, Tom Tinker, Chin Chopper: Fifty Musical Fingerplays.* Garden City, N.Y.: Doubleday, 1973.

Harrison, Annette. *Easy-to-Tell Stories for Young Children.* Jonesborough, Tenn.: The National Storytelling Press, 1992.

Justus, May. *Peddler's Pack.* New York: Henry Holt and Company, 1957.

Langstaff, John. *Hi! Ho! The Rattlin' Bog and Other Folksongs for Group Singing.* New York: Harcourt, Brace & World, 1969.

Leach, Maria. *Riddle Me, Riddle Me, Ree.* New York: Viking Press, 1970.

MacDonald, Margaret Read. *Look Back and See: Twenty Lively Tales for Gentle Tellers.* Bronx: H.W. Wilson, 1991.

_____. *Shake-it-up Tales.* Little Rock: August House Publishers, Inc., 2000.

_____. *Twenty Tellable Tales: Audience Participation Folktales for the Beginning Storyteller.* Bronx: H.W. Wilson, 1986.

_____. *When the Lights Go Out: Twenty Scary Tales to Tell.* Bronx: H.W. Wilson, 1988.

Meek, Bill. *Moon Penny . . . A Collection of Rhymes, Songs and Play-verse for and by Children.* Ossian Publications, 1985.

Miller, Teresa. *Joining In: An Anthology of Audience Participation Stories and How to Tell Them.* Cambridge, Mass.: Yellow Moon Press, 1988.

Pankake, Marcia and Jon. *Joe's Got a Head Like a Ping-Pong Ball: A Prairie Home Companion Folksong Book.* New York: Penguin Books, 1990.

Raffi. *The Raffi Singable Songbook: A Collection of 51 Songs from Raffi's First Three Records for Young Children.* Toronto: Chappell, 1980.

Schwartz, Alvin. *And the Green Grass Grew All Around: Folk Poetry from Everyone.* New York: HarperCollins Publishers, 1992.

_____. *A Twister of Twists, A Tangler of Tongues.* Philadelphia: J.B. Lippincott, 1972.

Shannon, George. *Stories to Solve: Folktales from Around the World.* New York: Greenwillow Books, 1985.

_____. *More Stories to Solve: Fifteen Folktales from Around the World.* New York: Greenwillow Books, 1989.

_____. *Still More Stories to Solve: Fourteen Folktales from Around the World.* New York: Greenwillow Books, 1994.

_____. *True Lies: 18 Tales for You to Judge.* New York: Greenwillow Books, 1997.

Sharon, Lois and Bram. *Elephant Jam: Songs to Play and Games to Sing.* Toronto: McGraw-Hill Ryerson, 1989.

Tashjian, Virginia A. *Juba This and Juba That.* Boston: Little, Brown, 1969.

_____. *With a Deep Sea Smile.* Boston: Little, Brown, 1974.

Taylor, Margaret. *Did You Feed My Cow?: Rhymes and Games from City Streets and Country Lanes.* New York: Thomas Y. Crowell Company, 1956.

Winn, Marie. *The Fireside Book of Children's Songs.* New York: Simon and Schuster, 1966.

_____. *The Fireside Book of Fun and Game Songs.* New York: Simon & Schuster, 1974.

_____. *What Shall We Do and Allee Galloo! Play Songs and Singing Games for Young Children.* New York: Harper & Row, Publishers, 1970.

Wiswell, Phil. *Kids' Games: Traditional Indoor and Outdoor Activities for Children of All Ages.* New York,: Doubleday, 1987.

Withers, Carl and Sula Benet. *Riddles of Many Lands.* New York: Ablelard-Schuman, 1956.

Withers, Carl. *A Rocket in My Pocket: The Rhymes and Chants of Young Americans.* New York: Henry Holt and Company, 1948.

_____. *A Treasury of Games.* New York: Grosset & Dunlap, 1964.

RECORDINGS

Baltuck, Naomi. *Crazy Gibberish.* Edmonds, Wash.: Traveling Light, 1993.

_____. *Crazy Gibberish Too!* Edmonds, Wash.: Traveling Light, 2006.

Beall, Pamela and Susan Nipp. *Wee Sing Silly Songs.* Los Angeles: Price Stern Sloan, 1982.

Fink, Cathy. *Grandma Slid Down the Mountain.* Cambridge, Mass.: Rounder Records, 1985.

Harley, Bill. *Monsters in the Bathroom.* Seekonk, Mass.: Round River Records, 1984.

Limeliters. *Through Childrens' Eyes.* Naperville, Ill.: Folk Era Records.

Nagler, Eric. *Fiddle Up a Tune.* Toronto: Elephant Records, 1982.

_____. *Improvising With Eric.* Cambridge Mass.: Rounder Records, 1989.

Raffi. *Rise and Shine.* Willowdale, Ontario: Troubador Records, 1982.

_____. *More Singable Songs.* Universal City, Calif.: MCA Records, 1977.

_____. *Singable Songs for the Very Young.* Willowdale, Ontario: Troubadour Records, 1976.

Sharon, Lois, and Bram. *Great Big Hits.* Toronto: Elephant Records, 1982.

_____. *Singin' 'n' Swingin'.* Toronto: Elephant Records, 1980.

_____. *Smorgasbord.* Toronto: Elephant Records, 1979.

Sterry, Anne-Louise. *Makin' Ravioli.* www.anne-louise.com, 2003.

ACKNOWLEDGMENTS

I would like to express my appreciation to all those who contributed their valuable skills, advice, and moral support to the writing of this book. Special thanks to Kaaren Moitoza Jacobs for her skillful transcription of the music; Cathy Andrews, who translated "May There Always Be Sunshine" into Russian, and her student, Anna Biahanskaya, who checked her translation; Scholastic, Inc., for permission to use "A Bed Just So" by Jeanne B. Hardendorff; Sharon Creeden for permission to adapt her version of "The Little Red House"; Gene Gousie, who introduced me to so many of these gems many years ago; Elly and Bea, who teach me the stretchers they learn at school and camp.

I would also like to thank Sharon Creeden, Pat Peterson, Margaret Read MacDonald, and Anne-Louise Sterry for their steadfast support, and Liz Parkhurst at August House for making it possible to turn a headful of songs and games into a book. I especially wish to express my heartfelt appreciation to all the storytellers, teachers, friends, and colleagues who have generously shared their favorite stretchers with me over the years.

"Let Me See Your Frankenstein." Traditional camp song. Back in the early 1980s, when I was head teacher at Community Day School, one of the kids, Heidi Tuttle, taught this to the teachers. I have never heard it anywhere else or seen it in print, but storyteller Katie Knutson told me that as a child, she learned it as a marching song.

"The Rabbits Are Eating the Tomatoes!" Traditional. My sister Lee Baltuck Carlson taught this to me several years ago at a family reunion. She had learned it from her kids. Another version, "Chickens Are in the Tomatoes," can be found in *The Great Rounds Song-Book* by Esther L. Nelson.

"One Hen, Two Ducks." My friend Carol Ranck learned this from her junior-high-school band teacher more than thirty years ago. My daughters and I invented the last of the ten verses to "round it off." I recently discovered a printed version, more traditional, in *A Bag of Moonshine* by Alan Garner.

"Zelda's Hammer." Traditional. I learned "Peter's Hammer" in 1995 in my daughter Bea's preschool co-op. I have also seen it as "Jenny's Hammer." I must confess that I changed the hammerer's name to "Zelda," which I find more ear-catching. A written version is included in Joanna Cole's *The Eentsy-Weentsy Spider: Fingerplays and Action Rhymes.*

"Does Anyone Know?" Traditional. I have seen several written sources for this, including *Miss Mary Mack All Dressed in Black: Tongue Twisters, Jump Rope Rhymes and Other Children's Lore from New England* by Scott E. Hastings.

"Uncle Joshua." Traditional. I learned this from a camper at the Bar 717 Ranch in 1977. I have seen it in folklore collections as "The Old Witch Is Dead" and as "Mary Died." A written source can be found in *A Treasury of Games* by Carl Withers.

"Montana Tex." Copyright © 1994 by Naomi & Deborah Baltuck.

"In a Dark, Dark Wood." This is my friend Gene Gousie's adaptation of a traditional English story. He added the music to involve audiences and an extra verse to accommodate the music.

"Skippin' Home from School." Traditional. I heard a Girl Scout leader tell this story around a campfire at an outdoor training session. I have also heard it told in prose and as a song, "Herman the Worm."

"Little Piggy Rap." Copyright © 2004 by Naomi Baltuck.

"A Bed Just So." Copyright © 1975 by Jeanne B. Hardendorff. Used by permission of Scholastic, Inc.

"The Little Red House." Copyright © 2005 by Naomi Baltuck. My friend Sharon Creeden's version of this story was my inspiration, and I thank her for her permission to freely adapt it.

"The Coffin." Copyright © 2000 by Naomi Baltuck. I first heard this traditional story in 1981 from my friend Gene Gousie. I adapted the story and tell it in the first person.

"The Dramatic Diagnosis of Doctor Drake." My sister Constance Baltuck Hartle told me this story. She said she learned it in Juneau, Alaska.

"Night and Day." This story was traditionally told by the Kittitas. A written version may be found in *Ah Mo: Indian Legends from the Northwest*, edited by Trenholme J. Griffin.

"Move Over." Traditional. A version of this song, titled "Marty," is included on the Limelighters' album of folksongs for children, *Through Children's Eyes.* In my opinion, this album, originally recorded in the 1960s, is one of the best recordings of children's folksongs available today.

"Teeter-Totter Woo!" Traditional. I first learned this story stretcher about fifteen years ago from a teacher and story-teller named Maryann, who was from Alaska. Several years ago I heard local Girl Scouts sing another version of this.

"Bazooka-zooka Bubble Gum." I learned this from my daughter Elly, who learned it at Girl Scout camp. I have never seen it in writing nor heard it anywhere else.

"Road Kill Stew." Traditional. My cousin Jean Bailey introduced me to this song. It is great for road trips!

"The Dickey Bird." I learned this at Girl Scout camp in 2001, but found a long-forgotten variant in my songbook from Camp Montecito-Sequoia in California, where I was a camp counselor in 1978. Last year, when I was in Denmark, I bought a CD of traditional Danish music said to date back to the heyday of the Vikings, and I was surprised to find a variant of this song chorus on it.

"Sardines!" I learned this song from Gene Gousie when we both worked at Montlake Community Day School. I have never seen or heard it anywhere else.

"Swing Low, Sweet Chariot." Storyteller Jay O'Callahan taught me the actions to this classic folksong more than twenty years ago. Some years ago, I called to ask him to refresh my memory, but he couldn't remember them, so I have invented new actions for those that I cannot recall. But I will never for-get the sight—it still makes me smile—of Jay singing *"sweet chariot"* while holding invisible reins to his invisible chariot and shaking as if he were racing it over huge cobblestones.

"Bill Grogan's Goat." Traditional, except for the last verse, which I wrote. I first learned this from Gene Gousie, my friend and co-teacher at Community Day School in the early 1980s. A written version of "Old Hogan's Goat" is included in Virginia Tashjian's *Juba This and Juba That.*

"I'll Tell My Ma." Traditional Irish folksong. I first heard this Irish street game sung by the Clancy Brothers at a St. Patrick's Day concert in Seattle. There is a written version in *Moon Penny . . . A Collection of Rhymes, Songs and Play-verse for and by Children,* by Bill Meek.

"Little Cabin in the Forest Green." Traditional. I learned this stretcher from Kathy Knutson, a co-teacher at Community Day School in 1981. I have never heard it sung anywhere else, but I did see a similar version on a Girl Scout song sheet.

"Hi-Ho-Jerum." Traditional. I learned this song from Gene Gousie in 1980.

"Pirate Ship." Traditional camp song. My daughter Elly learned this stretcher from a troop of Canadian Girl Guides at the Peace Arch Gathering in 2003.

"Ravioli." The melody is borrowed from "Alouette," a traditional French folksong. The words are traditional camp fare. A written version can be found in Alvin Schwartz's *And the Green Grass Grew All Around*.

"Little Green Frog." Traditional. My daughter Bea learned this song at a Girl Scout outdoor skills workshop. I had heard it years earlier, but it wasn't until I saw Bea sing it with all the accompanying motions that I thought it would be fun to learn and teach.

"Mrs. Murphy's Chowder." Traditional. I learned this song from Gene Gousie, but there is a written version in *The Fireside Book of Fun and Games* by Marie Winn.

"Purple Lights." I heard this sung at a Girl Scout spring encampment.

"Mmmm, I Want to Linger." I learned this from my daughter Elly, who learned it at Girl Scout camp.

"May There Always Be Sunshine." This song was written by a Russian schoolchild in the early 1970s. I first heard it performed by Michael Cooney in 1983 at the Alaska Folk Festival. My mother, Eleanor Baltuck, translated it into Russian for me, and I performed it in Russian and English for many years. I misplaced my mother's written version, but Mukilteo teacher, Cathy Andrews, was kind enough to translate the English verse into Russian for me.

"Keep Breathing." I learned this from my friend Kaaren Moitoza, who said it was adapted it from a lullaby sung to a child by its mother.

"Prinderella and the Since." This story was written by Frederick Chace Taylor under the pseudonym of Colonel LQ Stoopnagle and is included in his collection, *My Tale Is Twisted, or the Storal to this Mory* (New York: M.S. Mill Co, Inc., 1946).

"The Limerick Song." Traditional. I first heard this song in 1980 at a group singalong at Camp Long, a recreational facility of the Seattle Parks and Recreation Department, but I never knew the name of the group leader. A written version of this song is included in *Wee Sing Silly Songs* by Pamela Conn Beall and Susan Hagen Nipp.

"Tree Toad Trials." Traditional. There is no known author for this. A written version can be found in *The Biggest Tongue Twister Book in the World* by Gyles Brandreth. I recently heard storyteller Cherie Trebon sing this story at the Northwest Folklife Festival.

INDEX OF TITLES